Me Myself Milly

'...held my breath reading this bittersweet story
of sisters with secrets.'
Karen McCombie

'Clever, thoughtful and funny.'
Rosemary Hayes

Penelope Bush trained and worked as a tapestry weaver, and is the author of two highly acclaimed novels for teenagers, *Alice in Time* and *The Diary of a Lottery Winner's Daughter*. She lives in West Sussex with her husband and son and two mad cats. You can contact her via www.penelopebush.com.

Praise for *Diary of a Lottery Winner's Daughter*:

'Delightful . . . an irresistible read.'
School Librarian

'A good read for girls who are not quite ready for the disturbances of adolescence and are not sure that they are altogether comfortable with what it may involve.'
Books for Keeps

Praise for *Alice in Time*:

'An amazing book.
Cleverly written, exciting and fast-paced.'
Chicklish

'An ambitious and successful novel.'
Books for Keeps

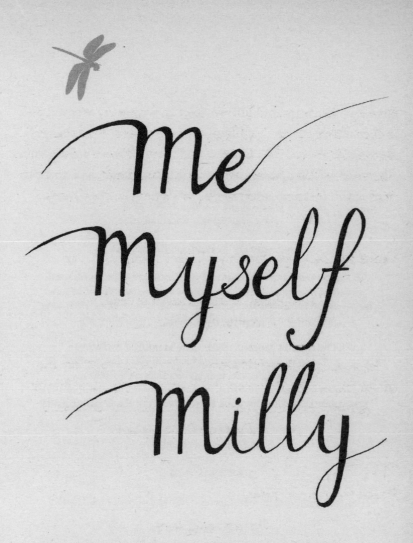

Me Myself Milly

PENELOPE BUSH

PICCADILLY PRESS • LONDON

First published in Great Britain in 2013
by Piccadilly Press Ltd,
5 Castle Road, London NW1 8PR
www.piccadillypress.co.uk

A catalogue record for this book is available from the British Library.

ISBN: 978 1 84812 252 9 (paperback)
Ebook also available

1 3 5 7 9 10 8 6 4 2

Printed and bound by CPI Group (UK) Ltd, Croydon, CR0 4YY

Cover design by Simon Davis
Cover illustrations by Carrie May

For Bushka
Thanks for the legacy

Chapter One

This week at the counselling session, Mr Jessop – or Ted, as he keeps telling me to call him – suggested I write a journal. He said it in that voice of his which he probably thinks is calming and hypnotic, but which is actually so monotonous I have trouble staying awake during the sessions.

'Milly, I think you should keep a journal; a private record of all your hopes and fears. Pour it all out on the page. Say what you're really feeling.'

Huh, what a joke. He's not saying what he's really feeling; what he actually means is, 'Milly, you come here to talk about what happened last April, only you won't, so I'm hoping you'll write about it instead and let me off the hook.'

Sure enough, he followed on by saying, 'Perhaps you

could write about what happened. You might find that easier than talking about it.'

Is he mad? Why would I write about it if I can't talk about it? I mean, when you talk, the words disappear into thin air; you say them and then they're gone. But when you write them down, they're solid, on the page, there for ever. I couldn't do that.

So when he tried to hand me a thick, spiral-bound, hardback notebook, I sat on my hands. He didn't take the hint and just stood there holding it out towards me.

It was pale turquoise, covered in tiny pink and green flowers and butterflies. It was pretty. And he looked so pathetic, I thought the least I could do was take it.

'I'll think about it,' I lied, shoving it into my bag, and then the timer on his cooker started beeping, which meant it was the end of the session.

I had no intention of writing a journal, but when I got on the bus to go home I started thinking about it. I wasn't even sure what a journal was. Was it like a diary?

Journal. It sounded like 'journey'. An account of some bloke's expedition to the frozen wastes of the Antarctic, maybe, that he wrote with frostbitten fingers, huddled in a tent while the wind whipped at the tent flaps. Or a woman in hopelessly uncomfortable Victorian clothing, fighting her way up the Amazon, clutching her leather-bound journal to her corseted bosom.

Both images, I realised, were from way back in the past when there was still some unknown corner of the globe to be explored. Not like these days when the whole world is there on Google Earth for everyone to see. I couldn't decide if that was sadly unromantic or wildly exciting. But, whatever, the word 'journal' sounded old-fashioned and a bit dusty, which was so typical of Ted. If I'd gone to the school counsellor, like the social worker suggested, she'd probably be telling me I should keep a blog.

A few weeks ago, the social worker they'd assigned to me after The Incident came round to say that she thought I needed to see a counsellor. Mum said we were fine, or would be if 'the authorities' would just leave us alone and stop sticking their noses in where they weren't wanted. Mum hates 'the authorities'.

No one mentioned Lily, who was sitting in the armchair in the corner with her legs tucked under her. But then, it wasn't Lily who needed a counsellor. It was me who needed one and I realised, at that moment, that this was the first time in fourteen years I would be doing something significant on my own, without Lily. It was such a huge, frightening thought, but I said, 'I want to go.'

Mum looked hurt but she couldn't really forbid me. Lily snorted in that derisive way of hers so I pretended she wasn't there. Things haven't been the same between us since The Incident. That's what I call the thing that happened last April – 'The Incident'.

She hates all the attention I'm getting but she can't do anything about it. It's not like I asked for any of it to happen. If anything it's her fault and she knows that, so she's keeping quiet. Which is weird for someone so noisy. It's spooking me.

The social worker was droning on about going to the school counsellor because she was good and it was convenient because I wouldn't have to travel. That's when I got to thinking about going back to school and I was seized with panic.

'Can I talk to you alone?' I said to the social worker. Mum took the hint – she's good like that, mad keen on giving us 'our personal space and privacy', and failing to see the irony. As a twin I never get any personal space, and privacy is also in short supply in our basement flat.

'I'll go and make some tea,' she said, leaving the room.

Lily didn't leave, even though I glared at her.

My social worker is called Carmel, which sounds suspiciously like 'camel'. As she has straw-coloured hair and large front teeth, it's an unfortunate name. Still, I'm hardly in a position to criticise first names as I was named after a muddy puddle.

I was still glaring at Lily, and Carmel glanced over at the armchair but she didn't say anything. That's another problem with being a twin. People tend to treat you as one person instead of two. Anyhow, I didn't really care if Lily heard what I was going to say. It was my decision and there was nothing she could do to stop me.

'I want to change schools – I want to go to a different school and I want you to help me sort it out.'

We both knew it was too much for Mum to cope with

at the moment. Lily snorted again but I ignored her. Now I'd had the idea and said it out loud, it had taken hold. I knew I had to do this if I was going to keep my sanity. Carmel didn't look so sure.

'I don't know,' she said. 'It's a big change, and I'm not sure that's such a good idea at the moment. What about your friends? You'll need their support . . .'

'No,' I cut in. 'I need a new start.'

I wasn't about to explain that apart from Lily there were no friends at school. Not really. That's another thing about being a twin: you're a unit and it sort of stops other people getting close. They assume you don't need anyone else. Besides, most other girls are a bit scared of Lily. She's so full on.

I half expected her to make a scene now, about me going to a new school without her. It was a mad idea; one I'd never have had before The Incident. But she must have known that one of her dramatic tantrums would have no effect on Carmel, so she didn't bother.

'Why don't you wait a bit, go back to school, see how you feel and then if you still want a change we'll see . . .'

'No,' I said again, surprised by my own daring. I'm not used to disagreeing with people or standing up for myself. Lily usually does that for both of us. But then a lot has changed recently and I suppose I'd better get used to it.

Carmel's a very forceful woman, though, and I knew that just saying 'No' wasn't going to be enough to convince her it was the right thing for me.

'Please,' I said, going for sympathy instead. So much for the new, assertive me. Carmel had been sent here by the police, as part of their Victim Support Unit, so really it was her job to help me.

'Please,' I said again. 'I can't bear the thought of people staring at me and pointing and whispering. They'll know what's happened, obviously. And I missed the whole of the summer term . . . I couldn't bear it, honestly. I really need a new start; somewhere I can just be me.'

I got the 'new start' idea from Archie's mum. I heard her talking to Jeanie upstairs about moving out. 'I think it's best,' she said, 'after all that's happened, that Archie has a new start and we can put it behind us.' I didn't blame her. It would be nice to walk away from it all, which is something I'll never be able to do.

Carmel stood up and Lily uncurled her legs and launched herself from the chair and from the room. She didn't look at me.

'I'll talk to some people and get back to you,' said Carmel. 'If you're sure it's what you want, I expect we can sort something out.'

'I'm sure,' I told her, though I wasn't. Not really. It was the first major decision I'd ever made on my own. Then Mum came back in and said she knew a really good counsellor who I could go to, so Carmel didn't need to worry about that any more. I could tell Carmel wasn't too happy about it. Perhaps she thought, like I did, that Mum was fobbing her off and there wasn't really any counsellor, but Mum was using her 'no nonsense' voice so Carmel didn't argue the point. But it turned out Mum was serious, which is how I ended up seeing Ted. And now he's given me a journal to write and although I don't want to do it, at least it's given me something new to think about.

I've spent the last however many weeks trying not to think, which of course is impossible. The more you try not to think about something, the more you end up thinking about it. The Incident has become like a film in my head, on a never-ending reel, that plays itself over and over. Sometimes it plays what actually happened and sometimes it plays what might have happened – what could have happened. I let that one play on, the one where we all come home laughing and happy. The one where nothing has changed us for ever.

My Journal
by myself, Milly Pond

This is my journal.

I don't know what I'm going to write yet, probably just anything – except what happened. I had decided I wasn't going to bother and I'd pretend I was doing it if Ted asked, but then I made the mistake of telling Mum about it.

When I got home from Ted's this afternoon, Mum was withdrawn and I could see she was feeling really down. In an attempt to distract her, I got the notebook out of my bag and told her about Ted's idea. It didn't cheer her up.

'What?' I said when she tutted loudly.

'I'm sure Ted means well . . . but really . . . he can't know much about fourteen-year-old girls if he thinks they're capable of keeping up a journal.'

I was offended. Why shouldn't I be capable? She might have been right if it was Lily she was talking to. I doubt she'd be able to do it; she's got the concentration span of a butterfly at the best of times.

I'm not going to tell Lily about the journal, she'll probably be even ruder than Mum and tell me to 'get a life' or something. Then she'll read it when I'm not here. I'll have to think of somewhere to hide it where Lily would never look. I can't put it under the mattress because that's too obvious. I think I'll keep it in the doll's house because Lily never goes near it. It sits on the chest of drawers between our beds and Lily wanted to get rid of it last year. She said it was embarrassing, that we were too old to still have a doll's house – but I wouldn't let her.

At first I couldn't think of anything to write. All those blank pages freaked me out so I did a sort of title page, like they have in books. 'The Journal of Milly Pond' sounded too formal so, in the end, I just put 'My Journal' right in the middle. Then, for some reason I added 'by myself'. I don't know why I wrote that and I wanted to cross it out but that would have made a mess so I put my name, Milly Pond, just to make things absolutely clear. Now it looks like something a six year old would have done. Anyhow, I'd filled a whole page, which felt good until I turned over and there was another blank page.

God! Who'd have thought writing could be so difficult? I don't know how Mum does it.

I must have sat here chewing on my biro for about half an hour before I decided that it doesn't really matter what I write because I don't think Ted wants to read it; I think he just wants me to write it. I'd better check though, next time I see him, just in case.

All that got me wondering about Mum. She writes and illustrates books for a living. I wonder if she panics when she sees a blank page. I doubt it; she probably sees it as an opportunity. I'll try and think like that from now on.

Chapter Two

Today, when I got home from Ted's, I stood on the pavement outside our house for a bit. I love the pavement. It's not plain grey like most pavements, it's made of big slabs which change colour depending on the weather, from pink to white to yellow and sometimes all three. And it's wide – wide enough for two ladies in huge, hooped skirts to pass without touching.

It rained earlier so the slabs are a mixture of yellow and pink. I half shut my eyes and tried to see the people who lived on the street when the houses were built. I have a pretty good idea of what the ladies would be wearing because I did a project on Georgian fashion last year, so I can imagine them parading up and down the street in their silks and satins on the arm of a gentleman. I tried to block out the cars that are parked all the way along the road and replace them, in my mind, with carriages and horses. That's the thing about living in a 'Historical City': the past is never very far away.

Lily hates it. She thinks people should move on and forget about the past.

Maybe she's right, I think, opening my eyes and facing the present. Our house is in a long row of identical sandstone houses that sweep down the street. If they didn't all have different coloured front doors I'd have difficulty finding the right one. Ours has got a black front door. It used to be red, which was much easier to spot, but the paint was flaking and the red had faded, so last year David painted it shiny black and fixed a new brass knocker right in the middle. He also painted the railings shiny black so now it looks really smart.

He offered to paint the grubby white door of our basement flat as well, but Mum said not to bother. I think he was a bit cross about that. Luckily, you can only see our front door if you stand against the railings and peer down.

I had my hand on the gate at the top of the steps that lead down to the basement area. I could see straight into our kitchen sink which was still piled up with the dishes from breakfast. Instead of going down I turned left, up the two shallow steps to the shiny, black front door. I do have a key to this door, but today it was unlocked so I let myself in. I was hoping Jeanie would be in; I couldn't face Mum just yet.

Jeanie was in the kitchen, which is at the back of the house. I could hear her humming along to the radio and emptying the dishwasher. Sometimes these days I can't believe this is the same house we've lived in since we were born. Everything has changed so much, and not just the black front door. Everything is shiny and new: the polished wood floors, the newly painted walls, the furniture, paintings – everything. I went past the door under the stairs which leads down to our basement flat. Even that's been painted.

Jeanie jumped when I entered the kitchen.

'Oh, Milly!' she said. There was a fraction of a pause, a heartbeat, before she said 'Hello'. I suddenly felt like I shouldn't be up here, at least not without an invitation. The thought made me want to cry. I could feel tears welling up. I must have gone red with the effort of trying not to let them fall.

'I'm just making coffee, would you like some?' Jeanie can always be relied on to say the right thing. Ever since The Incident she's never talked to me in that 'careful' way some adults do. She treats me like a normal person. So I sat at the breakfast bar and pretended to be a normal person for a bit.

Eventually, of course, I had to go downstairs. Opening the door to the basement and stepping through is like journeying to a different planet. The light which floods the upstairs, now all the walls are painted white, disappears beyond our door.

I descended the stairs carefully. It smells spicy with a hint of incense downstairs. It's not unpleasant and it goes with the decor which is all rich, earthy colours. There are hangings and paintings on the walls: Indian embroideries and dramatic stormy landscapes.

Every surface is covered with stuff. Stones are piled on shelves like pebbles on a beach after a storm. Of course every stone holds a special significance: a day out at the coast or an afternoon spent paddling in the river. There's a jam jar stuffed with feathers. Lily went through a phase of thinking that each time she found a feather on the ground it meant that an angel had been watching over her. There's a beautiful Victorian teacup with a penis-shaped cactus planted in it. Mum found them both at a car boot sale one Sunday morning. She said she'd love to have seen the faces of the Victorian ladies if they'd seen the phallic cactus sticking up out of their fine china.

It's like stepping back into the past because the whole house used to be like this, full of colour and throbbing with life. Not that it's exactly throbbing with life down here any more.

It was very quiet. I knew immediately that Lily wasn't here; it must be a twin thing. I don't know where she goes when she's not here and I'm not going to ask her.

I wondered if Mum was asleep. I was about to sneak into my room so I could carry on with my journal when I heard Mum call out.

'Lily?'

She was in the sitting room so I made my way in cautiously. She was curled up in the armchair wrapped in a blanket.

'It's me, Mum. Milly.'

Her eyes were unfocused. 'Oh, Milly. Yes, of course . . . sorry, I've just woken up.' She made an effort to smile. I noticed the bottle of pills on the side table, and surreptitiously checked to see that it wasn't emptier than it should be.

'You're only supposed to take these at night, Mum,' I said, picking up the bottle to get a closer look. It was okay, there was still over half left. 'I'll make you a cup of tea.'

'Milly?'

'Yes?' I stopped in the doorway, not wanting to face the mess in the kitchen but not wanting to talk to Mum either. She stared at me blankly. Whatever it was she had been going to say had fallen off the edge of her brain. I could see her trying to catch it on its way down – but it was gone.

'Thanks,' she said instead.

'That's okay, Mum. I won't be long.' I thought about asking her if she wanted something to eat but I didn't want to prolong the conversation. Besides, she'd only say no. I decided to make her a sandwich anyhow and hoped she would eat it.

While I was waiting for the kettle to boil I made a start on the washing up. Every time someone walked along the street I looked up, expecting the squeak from the gate followed by Lily's legs coming down the basement steps.

When I'd finished clearing up, I made Mum's tea and threw together a hummus and lettuce sandwich. I wasn't very hungry but I made a peanut butter and lettuce sandwich for myself. Mum's always been vegetarian so at home Lily and I are too, by default. If we eat out anywhere, Lily makes a point of ordering meat and if we do the shopping she always sneaks some bacon into the trolley and then stinks the flat out by cooking it until it's crispy. It's pretty gross really.

I was about to leave the kitchen, clutching Mum's

sandwich in one hand and her tea in the other, when I heard the gate squeak and the sound of footsteps coming down the stone steps.

Lily.

I put Mum's supper down and opened the door. It was Carmel.

'Hi, can I come in? I've got some good news.'

Reluctantly I let her in. I hoped I could keep Mum out of this. I didn't want Carmel to see her in a state. Carmel spotted the supper.

'Sorry if it's a bad time.'

I pulled out one of the chairs at the table, hoping Carmel would take the hint and we wouldn't have to go into the sitting room. But Mum must have heard the door.

'Lily?'

Oh God. Carmel looked at me enquiringly.

'Mum's just woken up; she's not too good today,' I explained. 'I'll just take her this sandwich, then I'll make you a cup of tea.'

'Okay, but she'll need to sign a few things,' said Carmel, putting her briefcase on one of the spare chairs.

When I got back from explaining to Mum that the social worker was here but she needn't worry about it, Carmel was making her own cup of tea. She indicated my peanut butter sandwich, 'Don't mind me, carry on,' she said, so I sat down and started on my sandwich.

'Right, the good news is, I've pulled some strings and managed to find you a new school.' She rooted around in her briefcase and came out with a folder. She didn't go on about how difficult it had been, with it still being the summer holiday and everything, but I sort of got the idea. To be honest I wasn't listening too closely. School isn't exactly my biggest priority at the moment. I just wanted her to tell me where it was and when term started. And I'd probably have to sort some uniform out. Beyond that I didn't really care. I know that sounds awful considering how much time I'm going to be spending there. But I made all the right noises, because I didn't want Carmel to think I was ungrateful. Eventually she got up to go, telling me she'd be back to talk to Mum about it later in the week and leaving me some forms for her to sign.

Finally, I got to my bedroom. I shut the door and turned on my bedside light. It doesn't do to turn the main light on. At least in the half dark I can pretend that Lily's side of the room isn't quite such a mess. One of these days I'm going to do something about it whether she likes it or not.

There's a sort of imaginary line down the middle. My side is tidy and her side is a tip. Her mess always finds its way onto my side of the room, mainly with clothes crossing the line, and I'm always pushing them back with my foot. Somehow my tidiness never encroaches on her side.

It's one o'clock in the morning and I'm beginning to wonder what I did before I got this journal. I asked Ted if he was expecting me to show it to him and he said, 'No, it's not like homework or anything. It's for you – you know – your private thoughts.'

I'm glad about that; it will make it easier to write and I love writing in it. Now I know why Mum loves her job so much – or did – she hasn't done much work lately.

At least she can sleep. Actually, that's unfair. She's only asleep at the moment because it's drug-induced. The doctor gave her something to help her sleep but he wouldn't give me anything. He said I was too young.

At first I liked sleeping because The Incident stopped playing itself in my head. Sleep was blissful unconsciousness. Is that even a word? I'll look it up tomorrow. So sleep was good, because you can't think when you're asleep. It's the waking up that's so hard. There's a few seconds when everything's okay, then the brain wakes up and reminds you about what happened and you realise you're in a waking nightmare. Then I started getting actual nightmares, so there was no escape, and now I dread going to sleep.

Reading is good because if you get a good book and really concentrate on the story, it's possible to get lost in it. But sometimes I realise I've read two pages without understanding a word because my traitorous brain has started thinking again, about what happened. I'm getting better at it though. Better at concentrating on the story. You wouldn't believe how many books I've read over the summer. I go to the library every Saturday and stock up. At first I stuck to the teen section but it's not very big so I had to move on to the adult section. I avoided the crime novels and had a go at the romance, but then I discovered action thrillers and they're the best because they move forward at such *a pace that you just want to keep reading. They don't give you time to think.*

And now I've got the journal.

The only problem is I can't write about my life because I don't have one at the moment, and I don't want to write about The Incident, so I've decided to write about Lily and me. I'll start when we were born, because it's a story we used to get Mum to tell us over and over. Lily always wanted to hear about how she'd been born first. I think she likes the thought that she occupied the world for a full five minutes without me.

It's funny to think we used to be the same person, or at least the same egg, before we split into two. We did it in biology and when the teacher was explaining it everyone kept staring at us like we were freaks or something, until Lily asked them what they were staring at and they stopped.

I wonder what it was like sharing a womb with Lily. Did we know the other one was there? Did we look at each other? Did Lily kick me? Was her side of the womb all messy? Ha ha.

It's almost impossible to imagine. I think I'll turn out the light now and try to imagine it; it might help me get to sleep.

Chapter Three

'Aren't you too old to be playing with doll's houses?' said Lily from the bed where she was sitting, cross-legged, watching me.

'I'm not playing.'

'Don't tell me, you're doing that weird thing again, aren't you?'

'It's not weird.'

She was referring to the way in which I use the doll's house as a sort of reference map. It's a replica of the house we live in, on King Street, and was made for us by Jason, an old boyfriend of Mum's, for our fifth birthday. It has a basement with three floors above and a red front door. I should probably paint the door black now, like David did with the real one.

There were eight dolls in the doll's house and each one represented an actual person.

Mum, Lily and I were in the basement, Jeanie and David on the floor above and Archie and his mum and dad on the floor above them. The only thing is, Archie's family moved out last week so I wanted to remove them from the doll's house.

I found the shoebox containing all the old dolls under Lily's bed and opened it. Inside were all the other people who'd moved out.

I picked up Jason. Jason was a Power Ranger out of a McDonald's Happy Meal. I don't know how we got hold of him because Mum would rather have done ten years in prison than taken us to McDonald's. Over the years the Power Ranger had stood in for whichever man Mum was seeing but I always thought of it as Jason because he was the first one I remember.

When we were little there were always lots of people living here. There was Jeanie and David, Finn and Holly – who were Archie's mum and dad, although Archie hadn't been born at the time – and Matt, Helen and Gina. Then Jason for a while and, although others came and went, these were our family – even if the neighbours referred to us as 'a commune'.

When we were five and Jason gave us the doll's house, there were two dolls inside. They were identical wooden dolls with round faces and long, curly, brown hair: Lily and me. We immediately demanded nine more dolls to make up the family. Of course we didn't get them, not all at once. We had to build up the collection slowly. The one we chose to

20

represent Mum was a plastic Disney Tinker Bell. We thought it suited Mum; she was just like a fairy with attitude. Eventually we had enough to represent everyone and although I'd stopped playing with them years ago, I liked to keep the right dolls in the doll's house. I knew it was weird but I couldn't help it.

'Get a move on then,' demanded Lily.

She watched me as I took Archie, Finn and Holly out of the doll's house and put them in the shoebox with Matt, Helen, Gina and Jason.

'Goodbye Finn, goodbye Holly – and good riddance Archie,' sang Lily as I dropped them into the box.

'Shut up!'

Lily folded her arms and looked sulky. She'd never liked Archie. She thought he was a snivelling mummy's boy. But I'd liked him. He was seven and a boy so he was bound to be a bit annoying at times, but I was going to miss him.

'It's your fault they moved out, so just shut up!' I said, glaring at Lily.

It was weird fighting with Lily. We never used to quarrel – well, not much, but ever since The Incident things have been different. It's like some huge black hole has opened up between us and instead of being two sides of the same coin – something people used to say about us all the time – now it's like we're two different coins, and not even in the same currency.

What makes me pick fights with her is the fact that I'm really mad at her and have been ever since The Incident. And

I hate being cross which makes me even more cross. It's a vicious circle and I don't know how to break it.

I picked up one of the twin dolls. Years ago, when we were about ten, we'd tied the hair back on one of the dolls and left the other one's hair loose. I was the doll with the ponytail. I picked up the one with the loose hair and stuffed it in the shoebox.

'What are you doing? You can't do that! It's cheating.' Lily was leaning over the side of the bed, trying to grab hold of the shoebox.

'Ha, so you do care, then.'

'No, it's just that you can't put me in the box – I'm here, aren't I?'

'Maybe if I put you in the box you'll disappear – like everyone else.'

'Now you're just being silly. Put me back.'

I looked at the doll's house. There was me and Mum downstairs and Jeanie and David upstairs. It looked horribly empty and wrong. I got Lily out of the shoebox and put her back.

I don't remember being born, obviously – that would be weird. But I've heard the story so many times it feels like a memory. I wonder if Lily feels the same way, although her take on it would be very different from mine. Lily knows how to make an entrance and even though, because we're twins, it was the same birth, it always seems to me that Lily was cast in the role of leading lady and I was the understudy. While she took centre stage I was waiting in the wings.

The story can't begin before that because there is no before that. Mum never talks about anything that happened before she came here and if she has any parents she's never mentioned them.

Mum's name is Summer and when she was in her final year at university she got careless at a music festival and found, on her return, that she was pregnant.

Mum was going through her New Age phase so, after she'd got over the initial shock, she gave thanks to the Great Earth Mother and didn't bother about going to see a doctor. Why would she? There was nothing more natural than childbirth and she was surrounded by her friends. Matt was a faith healer when he wasn't being the High Druid of the Somerset Pagan Worshippers, Helen was into crystals and had a crystal for every eventuality, and Finn's girlfriend, Holly, knew someone who knew someone who delivered all the babies born to the New Age travellers she used to travel with.

Mum took her pregnancy very seriously. She never let anything that wasn't one hundred per cent organic pass her lips, she stopped drinking coffee and she stopped smoking her 'herbal' tobacco. There were no scans or antenatal appointments. As she gradually expanded she knew that when the time came the Great Earth Mother would watch over her.

But as it happened, when she went into labour the Great Earth Mother must have been busy elsewhere, as was Holly's 'midwife' friend. Mum had hoped for a water birth in the big bath in the King Street bathroom. She lay in the bath, clutching one of

Helen's crystals and topping the cooling water up until all the hot water in the tank ran out.

By the time Holly, Jeanie and Helen were concerned enough to admit defeat and call for an ambulance, Mum was past caring. She just wanted the thing out of her.

The paramedics were brilliant. It didn't bother them that she didn't have any medical records. It was only after she'd been handed over to the hospital staff that the trouble began.

But Lily wasn't going to wait until they'd sorted out the lack of records or hitched Mum up to a monitor so they could check that everything was all right. Lily wanted out, so she waved me a cheery goodbye, or at least I like to think she did, and off she went. No doubt, from the depths of the womb I could hear the cooing and general celebrations that accompanied Lily's birth.

'Oh, what a beautiful baby girl, Ms Pond. Do you have a name for her?'

My mother's sweaty but serene face smiled up at them. 'I shall call her Lily.'

Summer Pond and Lily Pond – what could be more romantic?

'She's a bit on the small side but seems fine.'

'Hang on, there's another one in here!'

Lily's moment in the limelight was quickly cut short as she was whisked away to be cleaned and weighed and everyone turned their attention to the unexpected second baby. Eventually I was coaxed out and quickly shown to the now exhausted and shocked Summer before being whisked away to the intensive care unit and put into an incubator. I was just under five pounds in weight and a little on the yellow side.

What Mum wanted more than anything was to leave the hospital and get away from 'the authorities' who kept on telling her how stupid she had been and how lucky she was that her babies were okay. But she was tied by me, the unexpected baby, who was lying in the incubator. Not that the staff stayed cross with her for long. Mum looked so fragile and beautiful and hopelessly confused by suddenly having two babies to look after. And if she was sometimes too tired to make it up to the intensive care ward, Jeanie and David never failed to visit me twice a day.

So, while I concentrated on getting bigger and turning pink, Mum and Lily were left on the ward where they had plenty of time to get better acquainted.

Eventually Mum was allowed to take us home. There was one more obstacle to overcome, one more brush with 'the authorities' before normal life in the commune could continue: we had to be registered. David went with Mum to help out. She only had one baby sling so David carried me. Apparently I had no name up until the very last minute. Summer was determined to carry on the Pond-related theme but all she could think of was Mill Pond. Obviously, nobody is called Mill, but Milly was a perfectly respectable name. There was no time to consider the fact that maybe it wasn't such a good idea to have twins with rhyming names, or indeed that a mill pond didn't carry quite such romantic connotations as a lily pond. And so that's how I came to be named after a muddy puddle.

Chapter Four

Mum came with me today when I went to buy my new uniform. I was glad because as the beginning of term draws nearer, I'm getting really nervous about going to the new school. I had to buy a new blazer, jumper and tie. The new uniform is black and looks a lot smarter than my old maroon one. My new school is an all-girl's school, which means I'll have one less thing to worry about. And I was worrying. What if I can't make any new friends?

All through the shopping trip I was worrying about Mum being unhappy. I know I'm not as exciting or entertaining as Lily. I reckon she wished it was Lily getting the new uniform, Lily going on the shopping trip and going for coffee when we'd bought the things, but instead she was stuck with boring old me.

I really tried to keep cheerful, but it's hard to sound

natural when there's such a huge, unspoken thing hanging over your head. Mum was doing the same, so we were like two big fakes pretending to have a good time. Anyone would have thought we were just a normal mother and daughter out on a shopping trip, which is what we were trying to be. And failing.

I told Mum I wanted to go to the library before we went home.

When we got there Mum went off to talk to the librarians. She knows them all because she often does talks in there about her books. I couldn't get many books out, because I'd taken a load out on Saturday and hadn't returned them yet.

Actually, I only wanted one. It was called *How to Make Friends* and I didn't want to draw attention to it so I grabbed a couple of other books and hid it between them. I'm embarrassed that I need a book on something that most people do without even thinking, but the truth is that being a twin has made me socially inept and now that I've got to go to a new school on my own I don't know what to do.

When we got home I went to hang my new uniform in the cupboard next to Lily's maroon one. I try not to look at her clothes when I use the wardrobe. Her clothes are completely different from mine. She likes to look distinctive and original, whereas I like to blend in. They're a constant reminder of how things have changed between us. When we were little we used to insist that we wore identical clothes. Mum didn't approve, she kept telling us

27

we were individuals but we didn't believe her. We looked identical so we wanted to dress identically.

I was about to close the wardrobe door when my new tie fell onto the floor. I bent down to pick it up and caught sight of something stuffed into the back of the wardrobe that made my blood freeze. It was a blue hoodie. I didn't want it in my wardrobe but I couldn't bring myself to touch it. I slammed the door shut and put the tie away in my sock drawer. My heart was beating painfully fast.

I hid the library book about making friends in the doll's house with my journal. Just in time. I turned around as Lily came in. I'd never hear the end of it if she saw my book was *How to Make Friends*.

As it was, she was spoiling for a fight. She lay on her bed and smirked at me.

'I can't believe you're seeing a shrink.'

'I'm not.'

'Uh-oh, you're in denial,' said Lily, laughing.

'Ha ha, very funny,' I said, trying to give her a withering look.

I wasn't going to tell her that actually I'm enjoying my trips across town to see Ted. I like sitting on the bus, on my own. Nobody looks at me, or even notices I'm there. Not like when I'm with Lily. People always notice twins when they look so alike. They look in passing and then they look again. They usually smile. Lily loves it. She always looks right back with a smug expression as if to say, Yes, I was so amazing they made another one, just the same.

But on the bus no one knows who I am or what happened to me. The first time I got on the bus on my own I thought people would stare and somehow know – it was such a big thing inside of me it seemed impossible that the whole world couldn't tell. But nobody looked or whispered behind their hand, 'Hey, it's that girl, you know, it was in all the papers.' So now I like going out, I like the anonymity, though I worry about leaving Mum sometimes.

Mum's been a lot better today and I didn't want Lily to spoil it. She was in her workroom right now. Okay, so she wasn't working, she was just moving things around, but it was a big improvement.

'If you're not seeing a shrink, what are you doing then? Dating him?' Lily wasn't going to let up; she thinks it's hilarious. I wanted to point out it's all her fault but if I did she'd go away, and Lily in an annoying mood is better than no Lily at all.

'He's not really a shrink, we just sit in his kitchen and talk while he drinks tea.'

That was true. I wasn't sure that they were proper counselling sessions. I mean, Ted wasn't really a proper counsellor. Mum told Carmel she'd got me a counsellor but really he's just friend of Mum's from her university days who did a degree in psychology or something. Anyhow, he's very laid-back and we just sort of chat.

I think he used to worry that we weren't talking about what happened to me but now he's given me the journal he thinks I'm writing about it, so we talk about other stuff and never mention Lily or what happened. He's a lot more relaxed now, though that might be due to all the dope he smokes. He even offered me a drag once, though I think he was just being polite; he looked quite relieved when I said no. Ha ha, I'd love to see Carmel's face if she knew. I don't think that was the kind of therapy she had in mind.

But I don't tell Lily any of this, she'd just tell me I should have had some, like it's no big deal. We grew up around the stuff after all. I got quite nostalgic when Ted lit up. It reminded me of the old days in the house; the parties and the music. Lily and I would join in the dancing until we were so tired we'd fall asleep under the table.

Today Ted and I talked about books. I said I'd noticed that in a lot of children's books I'd read, like *The Lion, the Witch and the Wardrobe*, *Harry Potter*, *The Wolves of Willoughby Chase* and the Lemony Snicket books, the children's parents were either dead or conveniently not there. Ted said it was because at some point children want to believe they're autonomous. They want to grow up and move away from their parents and become their own person. Or their sister, I thought, though I didn't say it. I said I thought that in books it was probably more a case of getting the parents out of the way so the children could get on with the adventure without being called in for tea or told to wash behind their ears.

To be honest, I like talking to Ted. He doesn't treat me like an idiot and even if he does use words I don't always understand, I can look them up in the dictionary when I get home. Today I looked up 'autonomous'. The dictionary said:

Autonomy

i) the possession or right of self–government.

ii) freedom of action. From the Greek 'autonomous' meaning 'having its own laws'.

I like that. I am autonomous.

I didn't learn to talk until I was about four years old – at least not properly. Lily and I talked to each other but it was a weird, private language made up of sounds and gestures. I think, when we were younger, we each knew what the other was thinking and we didn't need to say it. If we had to communicate with adults, Lily did all the talking. She would say, 'We want a drink', or 'Milly needs the loo', so there was no need for me to talk. Eventually Mum realised what was happening and told everyone in the house they were to talk to me directly, not through Lily, and I wasn't to get anything unless I asked for it myself. These changes didn't bother me as much as they bothered Lily.

I discovered that I could talk, if a little quietly and hesitantly. This annoyed Lily, who quickly lost patience and tried to speak for me because she was so much better at it.

All I really remember about those early years is how Lily was always there. We played together, bathed together, even slept in the same bed. I think I thought I was Lily in a strange way. There was Lily and there was me, but in my head we were the same person. Mum had a big mirror on the wardrobe in her bedroom and we used to stand in front of it looking at ourselves. If I moved, Lily copied me, like a mirror in a mirror. I'd hold my left arm out, she'd hold her right arm out. The game was that she'd try and anticipate what I was going to do so that we did it at the same time.

Mum told us how, when she came to Bath as a student to study art, she soon got fed up with living in the student halls of residence so she and a few friends found the empty house on King Street and moved in. Mum said it was a beautiful house which deserved to be lived in and if the owner didn't care about it then they would. Lots of students came and went in the house, but Mum and her friends Jeanie, Matt and Finn were always there. Mum said, after they'd been living there for a couple of years, the property market really took off and the other residents in King Street began to complain about the squat on their doorstep. The council got involved and tracked down the owner. She was an elderly lady who lived in New Zealand but she was very ill and died, leaving the house to her great-nephew, David, who she'd never met. He was finishing his degree at Newcastle University and after he'd done his finals he came down to view his property and he never left. He fell in love with Jeanie and the house and the city; so Mum and her friends didn't have to move out.

When we were little there were about seven adults and three other children living in King Street. Mum had a theory that, although she'd given birth to us, we were humans, and one human couldn't own another human and, besides, the whole world was one big family, so we were to call her Summer

32

and not Mummy. *This didn't quite work out because when I was little I had trouble with my 's' sounds so I called her Mummer, which sounds like Mama anyhow.*

If we fell over and cried someone would pick us up and comfort us. If we wanted a bedtime story there was always someone willing to tell us one. And as the cooking was shared, a different person gave us our tea every night. If it wasn't always Mummer we didn't care or even notice.

Chapter Five

I was alone in my room, flicking through *How to Make Friends* and pretending that I wasn't panicking about starting at the new school next week. The book suggested that you should always act naturally. Well, that wasn't going to work. What if your natural self was painfully shy? I skipped over that bit and started on the chapter that talked about being optimistic and staying positive. How could I *stay* positive when I wasn't feeling positive in the first place?

It was hopeless. All the girls at the new school would already have friends that they'd made years ago and they wouldn't want some newbie barging in. Perhaps the whole idea had been a mistake. But then what were the alternatives? I really didn't want to go back to my old school and have people treat me differently, which they would. I wondered if I should persuade Mum to let me be home educated. But the thought of being stuck in the basement all day and never getting out was even worse. I'd just have to do it. There was no other choice. But, whatever, the library book wasn't much help so I stuffed it back in the doll's house. There was a knock on the door.

'Milly?' It was Mum. She didn't open the door and come in, which annoyed me.

'We've been invited upstairs for a meal with Jeanie and David. I think there's something they want to tell us. Five minutes, okay?'

'Okay.'

As I was brushing my hair I began to worry about what it was they could want to tell us. Were they planning on selling the house? They couldn't sell the basement flat, obviously, because that was ours, but there was no reason why they couldn't sell the rest of the house. It would certainly explain all the work they'd done on it recently. Oh God, I hoped it wasn't that. Or perhaps they were going to have a baby. That would be a good thing.

It turned out to be neither of those things.

Jeanie had cooked a lovely vegetarian curry and there was naan bread, poppadoms and chutney *and* yoghurt which kept us all busy, but I noticed that the atmosphere was a bit strained.

You know when something isn't being talked about and it's referred to as 'the elephant in the room'? Well, there was a whole herd of them in that room. You couldn't move for elephants.

David was obviously waiting until we'd eaten before telling us the news. Jeanie tried to start a conversation with Mum about her latest book, but Mum gave her a dark look and Jeanie backed off.

And then there was the biggest elephant of all, the daddy elephant: The Incident and all it entailed. So, all in all, it was an uncomfortable meal and a far cry from the meals that we used to have in this same kitchen in the good old days.

When we'd finished eating, David finally dropped the bombshell.

He explained that the university, where he lectures in English, had organised an exchange with an American lecturer, so he and Jeanie were going to move to Los Angeles for a year. It wasn't just a job swap, it would be a house swap as well; so that meant his American counterpart would be moving in upstairs and teaching here for a year. He said they'd be leaving in a couple of weeks. I felt sick.

Jeanie explained that the door between our basement flat and the rest of the house would have to be locked. Then she said I'd have to give my front door key back. I hate them. How could they do this to me?

David said it had been arranged for ages and they couldn't cancel and he was really sorry. He said he would have told us before but with 'everything that's happened' it never seemed like the right time.

I wanted to ask if they'd take me with them but I knew I'd just sound pathetic and Mum would never agree to it anyway.

I was desperately trying not to show them how upset I was,

but it must have been obvious because David put his hand on my shoulder and said, 'It'll be fun for you, Milly. They've got a son and he's not much older than you.'

Like that helped!

I made some excuse and ran downstairs so no one would see me crying. I cried into my pillow because I didn't want Mum to hear me. My pillow got all soggy and covered in snot so I turned it over and put it on Lily's bed. She'll never notice.

Eventually I stopped crying and lay on the bed following the cracks in the ceiling with my eyes. I felt strangely resolute. Like there was a piece of iron running through my body. Jeanie and David were going away. I'd just have to deal with it, like I'd dealt with everything else. It wasn't their fault – I knew that. So why did I feel that I'd been betrayed?

Why do people have to grow up and get sensible jobs and do their houses up and generally behave like adults?

I wasn't overreacting or anything. It was as if my dad had just said he was going away for a year. David is the closest thing Lily and I have ever had to a dad. Lily doesn't seem at all bothered and says she doesn't know why I'm making such a fuss.

I was so upset I opened the doll's house and took Jeanie and David out, even though they haven't left yet. I packed them in the shoebox and stuffed it under the bed.

When Lily and I were five we went to school. Mum had been planning to home educate us, but she'd started writing these books all about some twins which really took off and so we were sent to school after all.

We were the only twins in the school and, being practically identical, we caused a bit of a stir. At least Lily made sure we did. I say practically identical because, although we looked the same, we couldn't have been more different as far as personality went, so if we sat as still as statues and didn't say anything it was hard to tell us apart, but the minute we started to talk or move it was obvious who was who.

Lily liked to hold my hand all the time. She learned from an early age that people thought this was sweet. I remember the first day when the teacher put us on different tables. The girl next to me smiled and said she was called Becky. She showed me her new pencil case and then Lily was there, pushing her off the chair.

'That's my Milly,' she said and sat down. The girl started to cry and the teacher got cross and tried to get Lily to go back to her seat, but all she would say was 'My Milly', over and over again until the teacher gave up and let us sit together. It sort of set the scene for the next six years.

That was the time when Mum was seeing Jason. David was having an extension built on the back of the house so we could live in the basement and he hired Jason as the carpenter on the job. At that time we still mostly lived upstairs because that's where all the action was, but we had our bedroom in the basement and then Mum got her workroom down there so it sort of became ours.

Jason was working on the extension and of course he fell for

Mum; who wouldn't? I don't want to give the impression that Mum's had loads of men over the years because she hasn't – not really. Mum is very beautiful and she looks all fragile and vulnerable so men are always falling for her. The trouble is, although she looks fragile and vulnerable, she isn't either of those things. She's very strong and independent, so the sort of men that are drawn to her because they think they can protect and look after her soon discover that she doesn't need protecting or want to be looked after. Jason stayed around longer than most.

In our basement there are two bedrooms, a kitchen, a tiny bathroom, a sitting room and Mum's workroom at the back. It never used to feel small because we had the rest of the house as well, but since Archie and his mum and dad moved out there's been less excuse to go upstairs. And when Jeanie and David go we won't be able to go up there at all.

Sharing a bedroom with Lily never used to be a problem until recently. Just before The Incident Lily said she needed her own space and was going to ask Jeanie and David if she could have a room of her own upstairs. I told her Mum would never agree.

Chapter Six

I woke up really late this morning – in Mum's bed. For a minute I couldn't work out where I was and then I remembered that last night I'd had the most scary nightmare.

It started off with me looking at my reflection in a pool of water. I wasn't admiring myself or anything, I just caught sight of my reflection and thought, 'Oh look, it's me.' Then, as I looked closer I realised it wasn't me, it was Lily. I was outside looking at Lily who was under the water. And that's when it got scary because she couldn't get out and I was beginning to panic. We were staring at each other and there was this water in between us and then suddenly, like things happen in dreams sometimes, I realised it was me under the water, looking up at Lily and that's when I really began to panic.

I was holding my breath and I knew I'd have to breathe soon and I couldn't. The pressure was building up and up until

I couldn't hold on any more and I opened my mouth and water poured in and still I couldn't breathe and then I woke up and I was gasping for breath and shaking.

I switched the bedside light on, but the feeling wouldn't go away and in the end I went and climbed in next to Mum, like I did when I was little and I'd had a bad dream.

I decided it must have been an anxiety dream because of the new school and everything. I could still recall the feeling of panic, so I got up and showered and dressed in the hope that doing something would make the feeling fade more quickly.

Mum was in the kitchen with Carmel sorting out the final things for the school transfer. I poured myself a glass of orange juice and went to sit at the table with them.

Absently I picked up one of the documents that was lying there and didn't realise for a while what I was looking at. I knew it had to be my birth certificate but it couldn't be right.

'What's this?' I demanded of Mum.

'It's your birth certificate.'

I looked hard. It said Emily Pond, born 12th April.

'Why does it say Emily?'

Mum took the certificate off me and angled it towards the light. She looked hard at it, like I had.

'Mum? It says I'm called Emily.'

'I can see that,' said Mum. I couldn't believe how calm she was.

'How come no one ever told me?'

'The thing is, I don't really remember,' said Mum. 'When

we went to register you I wasn't really myself. I think I was in shock, you know – I wasn't expecting two babies . . .'

Typical, blame me, why don't you. It was a pretty lame excuse.

'You could go and ask David. I think it was his idea. But what does it matter? You'll always be Milly.'

I had been planning to avoid David after his bombshell about going to America but I could make an exception for this. I paused in the doorway though and said to Carmel, 'Make sure you fill in all those forms with Emily – not Milly.'

Carmel looked up. 'But I've already done them.'

'Well, do them again,' I said and stomped up the stairs in a way that I hope conveyed the message, 'Don't mess with me.'

David was finishing off the new shower room which he'd just installed in the small room right next to the door that led down to our flat. It had always been used as a large cloakroom where all the coats and boots and outdoor wear were kept. There'd been loads of things in there and if it was cold and you needed to wrap up you just grabbed what was handy. But in the renovations that had taken place it had been made into a downstairs loo with a shower. David was fitting the glass door onto the shower cubicle.

'Yes, I vaguely remember,' he said after I'd explained about the recent discovery.

He had a couple of bolts in his mouth so it was all a bit mumbled and he had that far away expression people get when they're trying to remember something.

Vague wasn't going to cut it.

'David!'

'Oh, right,' said David, taking the bolts out of his mouth and putting the screwdriver down. 'I was just about to stop for tea. Let's go into the kitchen.'

'As far as I remember,' said David as he filled the kettle, 'your mum was dead set on this Pond business, you know – having a name that went with your surname. She had Lily all lined up and then you popped out and she was a bit stuck. Anyway, when we got to the registrar's office I thought you should have a proper name.'

David was smiling at me. I know he's always had a soft spot for me. In fact, I'd go as far as to say I was his favourite. Now I understood why.

'Don't get me wrong, there's nothing wrong with Milly. It's just that it sounds like it's short for something else.'

'You mean, more like it's long for Mill, as in Mill Pond!' I said bitterly.

'Yes, well . . . don't blame your mum too much; she was in a bit of a state . . .'

'Yeah, I know, she went into shock when I appeared!'

David laughed. 'You have to admit, it was quite funny. But you were the sweetest little thing – so different from Lily . . .' He trailed off. Looked embarrassed. I steered him back onto the subject of my name.

'So you persuaded Mum to call me Emily?'

'I persuaded her to register you as Emily. She was always going to call you Milly.'

I went round the table and gave David a hug. 'Thank you,' I said.

David hugged me back. 'Glad you like it. It was a toss up between Millicent and Emily.'

'I'm glad you picked Emily, I love it.' I let go of him and he went to get the milk out of the fridge. I sat back down at the table.

'I can't believe no one ever mentioned it!' I said.

'It was only me and your mum who knew,' David said. 'And as far as your mum was concerned you were Milly, so I guess I didn't mention it again and then I sort of forgot. Sorry.'

'It's okay,' I said, 'in fact it's perfect. I'm glad I've only just found out.'

I went back downstairs and looked up the meaning of my name on the internet. It said: *Emily – from the old Roman family name Aemilius, meaning 'rival'*. Ha ha, I can't wait to tell Lily.

I can't believe what's just happened; I've got a new name! Just as I was having to become a different person I get a whole new name to go with it. I woke up this morning as Milly and now I'm Emily!

I know it might sound daft and nobody else seems to think it's a big deal, but it is to me.

We don't know who our real dad is.

Mum met him at a festival and they'd had better things to

do than exchange personal details, so all she knew about him was that he went by the name of Shaggy. *So apt in so many ways*, Mum used to say, whatever that means.

Lily and I used to dream of one day finding Shaggy and telling him we were his twin daughters. It didn't seem right that somewhere there was a man wandering around who didn't know he was our dad.

When we were ten Lily and I decided it was our duty to find this man and inform him of his good fortune. We imagined the scene, sometimes even acting it out. Lily always played the part of our father because it required a great deal of emotional acting and Lily was better at that sort of thing than me.

Sometimes we pretended we'd tracked him down and we acted out the scene where we knocked on his door and told him who we were. Or we'd pretend we were on a train and we'd overhear a man telling his friend how he'd met the most beautiful woman called Summer at a musical festival years ago but he'd never been able to forget her. We'd then reveal our identity and it would all end in joyful tears.

We pestered Mum for every small detail she could remember about him. Then we bought a big scrapbook and wrote them all down carefully. When we'd finished we had covered half of the first page. This is what we had:

Shaggy:
- about twenty-five (ten years ago – so mid-thirties now)
- about five foot eleven
- hair and beard – long, brown and curly – like our hair

- *accent – not really, might have been to public school but was covering it well*
- *had a friend called Spikey or Spidey or something like that*
- *liked pickled onions and real ale (apparently not a good combination when you're sharing a tent)*
- *distinguishing marks – none, no tattoos or weird-shaped birthmarks*

That was all we managed to get before Mum twigged what we were doing and gave us the lecture on how our father, while important in our conception, was not important in any other respect. Traditional family units were redundant in this day and age and we were well provided for as we lived in a communal household. This was true, at the time there were seven adults and five children in the house on King Street, but none of them was our father. What made it harder was the fact that we don't look like Mum so therefore we must look like him.

In the absence of any information about our real father and the fact that we had a whole scrapbook to fill, we took to finding and cutting out any photographs of men that even vaguely fitted his description. Which turned out to be pretty much anyone with brown hair. We got pictures of actors and rock stars as these were the easiest to come by. Then we moved on to catalogue models and politicians and TV presenters. By the time the scrapbook was nearly full I felt I should point out to Lily that our dad might not be in the public eye. He might be a normal man whose photo had never appeared in a magazine or paper or on the internet.

Lily didn't like the idea but she had to agree it was possible, so we moved to plan B which was to take pictures of likely looking men with Mum's camera.

To be honest we didn't find very many. Lily refused to accept that he'd had any other children, so men with families weren't allowed. But we got a few; not many people notice where children are pointing their cameras. Lily would stand as close as possible to the man in question without looking suspicious and then I would pretend to be taking a picture of her. This had the added bonus that when we printed the picture off we could immediately compare him to Lily to see if there was any family resemblance.

Of course, eventually Mum found the scrapbook and realised what we were doing, so she sat us down for another talk. She looked really unhappy.

'Listen,' she said, 'I'm really sorry that I don't know who your father is and I'm not proud of the fact. I think you need to accept that there's no way of finding him and there's no point in thinking about him; you'll drive yourselves mad if you spend the rest of your lives thinking he could be that man in the street or so and so on telly. Please let it go. You'd be much better off thinking about what you do have, rather than what you don't have. You've got me and each other and that's enough. It has to be. Okay?' She was close to tears and so Lily and I agreed that we'd let it drop. And we mostly did; only I still find myself wondering whenever I see a man with brown, curly hair.

Chapter Seven

New school today. At first I pulled the duvet over my head and wondered if anyone would notice if I didn't get up. Ever again. It just all seemed too much.

When I peered out, five minutes later, Lily was staring at me from her bed. She hasn't said anything about the fact that I'm going to a different school. I don't know why; I don't know if she's cross, or jealous, or what. But she must have realised how worried I was and didn't gloat over my predicament.

'Don't think about it, just do it,' she said.

I grinned. It was Mum's favourite saying when there's something unpleasant to be done.

Don't think about it, just do it.

That got me out of bed, then I focused on the things I needed to do like have a shower, get dressed and take Mum a cup of tea. I was so busy focusing that, when Mum sat up to drink her tea, I said without thinking, 'Are you going to do some work today?' Big mistake. Mum shut down.

She had a deadline on the latest book but she hadn't done any work on it since April. I knew the publisher had cut her some slack, but it was worrying. What if she had that writer's block thing? We might be able to live on the money from the other books, but I didn't really know. Anyhow, it was obvious that now was not the time to talk about it.

Lily and I parted at the basement gate. She watched me all the way down the street until I turned the corner. I couldn't believe I was doing this. It hurt. You know when someone loses an arm or a leg in an accident and you hear stories about how they can still feel it, even though it's not there any more? That's sort of how I felt – like I'd lost Lily but she was still there. Even when I was walking down the street on my own, she was still with me. Which was crazy, because the whole point of this was so I could learn to stand on my own two feet.

What did I expect? That I was going to be able to follow her around for ever more? People grow up. That thought caused a gigantic lump in my throat and I thought I was going to start crying. That would be great: standing at the bus stop, all alone, crying. I could see a few girls at the bus stop in the same uniform as me, which brought me back down to earth. I tagged on the end of the queue and tried to look as inconspicuous as possible.

My plan was to stay that way. Inconspicuous. I'd studied

How to Make Friends, and although the book made it all sound easy I knew it wouldn't be. So I'd decided not to bother. Who needs friends anyway?

If things got really bad I could pretend Lily was with me. It couldn't hurt, just for a bit. Until I'd settled in. On the bus I sat alone and held an imaginary conversation with Lily. In my head, obviously.

'That girl over there looks even more scared than you,' said Lily.

'Do you think I should go and talk to her?'

'No. Not your problem. Anyhow, if she's scared she can't help you.'

'I'm not scared.'

'Yes, you are.'

'Okay, maybe just a bit.'

'Try and focus on something else.'

'Like what?'

Silence. It was a stupid idea anyhow. Lily wasn't here. I was in danger of crying again. I am so pathetic, I thought. What's wrong with me? I've got to get this under control. I took a deep breath.

'I am Emily. I am fourteen. I am a normal girl going to school, like any normal girl. If anyone asks, my name is Emily.' It felt weird, like trying on someone else's shoes. But that's who I was now: Emily. What was Emily like? Quiet, but not boring, I could be fun, just not yet. I hated getting into trouble so I would be keeping a low profile. And, above all, I didn't need anyone else. I would be self-contained.

The bus stopped and all the black-and-white clad girls piled out, chattering like a load of magpies.

One for sorrow.

Stop it!

They wandered off in a flock, towards the school. I followed, but at a distance. So did the scared-looking girl from the bus. She drew level.

'Hi, my name's Stephanie but everyone calls me Effy.'

It was as if she'd swallowed *How to Make Friends* whole. I thought about ignoring her but it would've been rude and besides I wanted to try out my new name.

'Emily. My name's Emily Pond.'

'So what's this school like then? I used to go to St Bart's, but my dad's business collapsed and he can't afford it any more. It was me or the house, although actually we might lose the house as well.'

I didn't know what to say to any of that. I'd known her precisely two minutes and I already knew her life story. She didn't sound bitter or sad about it; she was quite chirpy, like it was all a great new adventure. As it happened we'd reached the school by then so I didn't have to say anything.

'I have to go and report to reception, because I'm new,' said Effy.

'Same here,' I said as we went in through the doors.

'Really? That is *so* brilliant! Which year are you in? I'm in year ten – please tell me you're in year ten.' I told her I was. I thought she was going to hug me so I backed off slightly, trying not to cringe. She was probably just chatting like this because she was nervous, I decided.

Effy's voice was very loud and I wanted to tell her to keep her voice down and not draw too much attention to herself, or me for that matter.

In fact, I was so concerned about her, I forgot to be scared. I looked around the entrance hall. It was massive, like an airport or something. The whole school was brand new. Or nearly – it had been built about three years ago and it was all state of the art. Not like my last school, which was old and depressing. Of course, that made me think about Lily again and I really didn't want to cry.

'Wow, look at this,' said Effy. 'It's nothing like St Bart's. That was practically falling to bits compared to this,' which made me laugh because I knew that St Bartholomew's was a very exclusive, fee-paying girl's school and was housed in a Georgian mansion in its own grounds on the outskirts of the city.

So I was feeling better by the time we were taken into an office and given maps and a list of rules and stuff like that. There were six new girls, not counting all the new year sevens who were being dealt with separately. Some looked older than me and some younger. Effy was the only one who looked about my age. Then a woman called out, 'Stephanie Wright and Emily Pond.' We put our hands up and moved over to where she was standing. 'Follow me, you're in 10FE. I'll show you the way, but pay attention. You'll have to find it on your own tomorrow.'

We followed her down a corridor, up some stairs, then

turned left, through some double doors, down a corridor, turned right, down another corridor, turned right again and there it was. The woman opened the door and ushered us in.

It wasn't as bad as I'd thought it was going to be. I think I'd imagined a roomful of fourteen-year-old girls who all stopped what they were doing and stared at me, maybe whispering behind their hands and giggling about 'the new girl'. But what actually happened was that, although a few people looked up, they soon went back to what they'd been doing. I realised that it was a mixed tutor group. In other words they had different year groups from seven to eleven. Years twelve and thirteen must have their own room somewhere. I found a seat and started to draw on my map the route we'd just walked. I didn't want to get lost tomorrow.

Effy came and sat next to me. I noticed she was a lot quieter than she had been. She wanted to compare timetables with me to see how many lessons we had together. We'd already made our GCSE choices at our other schools and they were surprisingly similar so we had most of our lessons together. She looked so relieved I had to laugh. I felt a bit sorry for her; coming from St Bart's it was going to be hard for her to adjust.

When we were eight I got an invitation to a party. It was from Becky, the girl I'd been put next to on my first day at school. She thrust it at me as we were putting our coats on. We knew what it was because there were balloons printed on the front of the envelope and all the way home Lily was getting excited because she loved parties. It wasn't until we were at home that I opened it and discovered that it was only addressed to me. Lily wasn't invited. Her face fell. I started to cry. I was crying because I felt bad for Lily.

Mum came to see what all the fuss was about.

'Never mind,' she said when she found out about the party. 'It can be your first lesson in being an individual.' I didn't know what she meant and Lily still looked cross and upset.

Later, in our room, I said to Lily, 'I don't want to go to the stupid party.' I did but to say anything else would have been disloyal. It was a Pamper Party and we were going to get our nails painted and our hair done and even try out make-up but how could I enjoy all that when I knew Lily was all alone at home? We were sitting on the bed and Lily had her arm around me. She didn't like it when I cried.

'It sounds awful,' she said, looking at the invitation.

'I know,' I lied. 'I don't even like Becky,' I added for good measure. This wasn't true; I did like Becky, she was nice but she'd left us alone since Lily had pushed her off the chair. I only said it because I felt bad about how much I wanted to go to the party, so I thought, if I pretended it was a big ordeal, Lily wouldn't mind so much or be cross with me.

'Don't worry,' said Lily, 'you don't have to go.' She was right. It would be better if I didn't go at all. I tried to keep the disappointment out of my voice and said, 'Let's go and tell Mum I'm not going.'

'No, we can't do that. She thinks it's a good idea and you

don't want her to think that you're bottling out of doing something on your own. No, it's simple – I'll go for you; Becky will never know the difference.'

So that's what happened. I was so swept up in Lily's secret plan, and how funny it would be to trick everyone, that it wasn't until Mum pulled up outside Becky's house and Lily jumped out of the car that I realised it was me who was now missing the party and Lily who was going to have all the fun. All week I'd been grateful to her because she was 'doing this for me', as she kept reminding me if I'd had any misgivings.

'Right then, Lily,' said Mum from the front of the car. 'It looks like we've got an afternoon to ourselves. Let's have some fun.'

I felt momentarily jealous. Mum was looking forward to having Lily to herself. But it did mean that I was going to have Mum to myself, even if she thought I was Lily, which was some consolation.

'What would you like to do?' Mum was asking.

I wanted to say we should go home and have our own pamper party or go and get our nails done at a real nail bar, but as Lily had spent the whole week saying pamper parties were lame and who'd want their nails done anyway, it wasn't really an option. I had to remember I was pretending to be Lily. What would Lily have chosen? Shopping probably. But I was worried about keeping up the pretence of being Lily. Lily talked a lot and already I couldn't think of anything to say.

'Lily? Are you all right?' said Mum. Oh no, she was going to notice and Lily had only been gone two minutes.

'Let's go to the cinema!' My voice came out far too loud, but then Lily was loud so that was okay.

So we went to the cinema and I remembered to ask for a mint choc chip ice cream even though I wanted a strawberry one. When Mum asked me which film I wanted to see, I said *Pirates of the Caribbean* because I knew Lily wanted to see it. I was so relieved when Mum said it was rated 12 and why didn't we go and see *Brother Bear* instead that I didn't object like Lily would have done.

When the lights went down I breathed a sigh of relief. This had been a brilliant idea. Sitting next to Mum in the dark I couldn't go wrong, even though it seemed a waste of having Mum to myself for the first time.

When we picked Lily up from Becky's house she had blue nail varnish on, her hair was up in an elaborate style, she had gold glitter on her cheeks and shoulders and a painted-on tattoo of flowers and leaves on her foot. She took her shoe and sock off in the car to show me. I would have chosen pink nail varnish.

She was so excited she couldn't stop talking or showing off the tiara she'd won in the Catwalk game. I was sure I wouldn't have won that game. I had to glare at her to get her to calm down.

When we got home and were sitting round the table, Mum said, 'So, Lily,' looking at Lily with her hair and nails all done and not at me, 'Do you think Becky knew it was you at her party and not Milly?'

Lily looked guilty and sulky at the same time. 'When did you realise?' she asked.

'About two minutes after you got out of the car,' said Mum.

That night when we were in bed, Lily said, into the darkness, 'That was the best party I've ever been to.'

On Monday, at school, Becky came up to us and asked me if I'd enjoyed the party. 'It was the best party I've ever been to,' I told her and she smiled slyly over my shoulder at Lily. Lily just smiled right back.

Chapter Eight

I stayed on the bus after school because I was going to Ted's. Effy wanted to know where I was going so I told her I was going to see a friend. No way was I going to tell her I was seeing a counsellor.

It's easy being with Effy because she does all the talking. I was wrong about her swallowing *How to Make Friends* because there's a whole chapter in there on how you shouldn't talk about yourself all the time, you should engage with the other person and ask them about themselves and find out what interests them. Luckily Effy doesn't do any of those things.

When I told her I was going to see a friend she started going on about how difficult it was to stay in touch with her old friends and how it's like they don't want to talk to her now she doesn't go to their school any more. I was glad she was talking, though, because it meant that I didn't have to.

Ted asked me how the journal was going. I told him I'd made a start and that I was writing about Pond Life. He looked momentarily confused, probably thinking I meant newts and frogs and stuff, then it dawned on him that Pond is my surname.

'Right!' he said. 'That's cool.'

When Ted says 'cool' he does not say it in a cool way. He says it slowly and draws it out like some stoned hippy. It made me want to giggle.

I told him about my 'new' name, Emily, and how I've had it all these years and never knew. He looked as if he was about to say 'Cool' again but he changed his mind. Then he asked me if it made me feel like a different person. I had to think about that for a while.

'Sort of,' I told him. 'It's weird, I feel like the same person, only different.' Ten out of ten for clarity. I tried again. 'No, it's not the name that makes me feel different. I mean, I *am* different since . . . you know.' Ted nodded. 'So it sort of feels right that I get a new name to go with the . . .' I didn't want to say 'new me'. It sounded wrong. 'New' sounded good and I didn't feel good. '. . . different me,' I finished.

He asked me about the new school.

'It sucks,' I said.

I don't have to pretend with Ted. He didn't ask me in what way it sucks, he just waited for me to tell him.

'I feel like a fake. I keep expecting to see Lily, only of

59

course she's not there, and half the time I want to explode – I want to shout that I'm a twin, that I'm only half a person. No one there knows about Lily – they think I'm just me.'

'You are "just you",' said Ted tentatively.

'I know! It's just that all my life I've been one half of a pair – Lily's twin – and now suddenly, at this new school, I'm not. That's why I feel like a fake, like I'm pretending to be someone I'm not.'

It was so hard to explain, especially to someone who isn't a twin. Of course, you know that you're your own person. It's just that somehow you're more than that. You're an individual but you're also a pair. Suddenly being just an individual is scary. Lily defines me in some way. It's not that I'm sorry I've gone to the new school where nobody knows about her. It's just that it's going to take a bit of getting used to.

'Why haven't you told any of your new friends about her?'

I thought about Effy and how she never stops talking long enough for me to tell her anything, and how she's permanently cheerful no matter what life throws at her.

'Because it would change how they see me. I need to be *me*. I guess I'll get better at it.'

On the bus home I struggled to stay awake. All I wanted to do was close my eyes and go to sleep but I was scared I'd miss my stop. I nearly fell asleep in maths today because I had another nightmare last night. What I needed was a good night's sleep. I wondered if I'd ever have one again. I seriously considered nicking some of Mum's pills; I doubt she'd notice. The trouble is I've seen how groggy she is in the mornings and if they made me like that then there's not much point.

The bus stopped at the lights right next to a bookshop. They had a whole window display of Mum's 'Twins' books with the dolls and everything. A couple of years ago Mum's twin stories were made into a television series. Lily was mad because she wanted us to play the twins but the twins in Mum's stories are boys.

I think she did that so Lily and I wouldn't think she was writing about us. Thank God she did. I'd hate people to think that.

The books are for younger children and the TV series was a great hit. In the end they did it in cartoon form and they brought out a couple of dolls to go with it. We used to have some but I think Archie took them with him when he left.

Mum bought the basement off Jeanie and David with the money. I'm really glad she did because I'd feel uncomfortable living there now if it still belonged to David; like we'd outstayed our welcome or something, now everyone else has gone and with the Americans coming.

When I got home Mum wanted to know all about the new school. I told her it was the best. She wanted to know if I'd made any new friends, so I told her about Effy because I didn't want to worry her. And besides, Effy seemed to have decided I was her new Best Friend. She gets off the bus a stop after me. She lives behind the park which isn't far away because it's not a very big park, more like a garden really.

Lily wasn't around so I wandered upstairs after tea to see Jeanie and David. They're going next week and I wanted to make the most of being able to go up while I still can.

It's just as well they've made all the changes up there, because they wouldn't have been able to house swap with the Americans if it was still falling apart and full of random people.

Jeanie and David wanted to know about the new school as well. They said it sounded good and they'd be back in time for my GCSEs so I wasn't to worry.

Jeanie said she was trying to get a room ready for the American couple's son but she wasn't sure what he'd want and perhaps I could help her. I didn't have a clue and I told her so. What did I know about boys?

David said, 'I know you're upset with us for going away, Milly, and I'm really sorry it had to happen now. But please don't take it out on the Americans. Be nice to them, okay?'

'Of course I'll be nice,' I said, offended. Then, to convince him I meant it, I politely pumped them for information about the son. Not that I was interested or anything.

They told me he's called Devlin. He's nearly sixteen and he's not going to school here; he's going to study from home on the computer and stay in contact with his American school.

This sent David off on a long explanation about how he's had to get Wi-Fi fitted and how he's bought a new computer for them to use because he doesn't want them using his PC while they're away and would it be rude if he was to lock his study door for the duration.

'Yes, it would,' said Jeanie. 'You'll just have to remove all your personal stuff. We can lock the attic, they won't need to go up there.' I left them to it and went back downstairs.

Lily was in the kitchen. She didn't ask me about the new school. I got my homework out and she disappeared. Which was fine by me.

I've just remembered. I did have to go to school on my own once. It was when we were ten and just before we left the house Lily started throwing up. As Mum was holding her over the sink – because she'd started really suddenly and didn't have time to get to the bathroom – she saw Daisy and her mum walking past on the street above. Mum sat Lily in a chair, opened the door and called up to Daisy's mum, asking her if she'd take me to school so she could stay behind and look after Lily. It all happened so quickly that neither Lily or I had time to object and before I knew it I was at school, on my own. When I sat down next to Lily's empty seat I felt sick and wondered if I had the same bug as Lily. I kept thinking if I threw up Mum would have to come and get me, but however hard I concentrated on being sick it didn't happen. By break time I'd got over my nerves and felt okay. I wandered out into the playground looking for someone to play with. I could see Daisy and Becky under the tree and was about to go and join them when my path was blocked by a big object. Hayden, the meanest boy in the school, was pushing his face into mine. I backed up and tried to go round him but he kept sidestepping and blocking my way until he'd forced me round the back of the old toilets.

'You're Milly, right?'

I nodded and couldn't help looking round for Lily even though I knew she was at home.

'What do you want?' I said, as boldly as I could.

'What do you think?' he sneered.

I had no idea what he meant so I just stared at him. Then it dawned on me. He must want a kiss or something. Yuk! Still, if it meant he'd leave me alone I supposed I'd have to get it over with. I darted forwards and gave him the briefest kiss on the cheek that I could manage. Hayden went bright red. I remember wondering why he was embarrassed when he'd asked for it. But it turned out it wasn't embarrassment turning him red, it was rage.

'God! Get off me, you freak!' he yelled in my face. Then he grabbed my arm and started twisting it. I thought it was going to snap. 'You bring it tomorrow or next time I'll break it,' he said, letting go of my arm. 'And don't even think about telling your sister.'

I was shaking and I wanted to ask him what exactly it was that I was supposed to bring him tomorrow but I couldn't get the words out.

'Do you get it?' he yelled, covering me in a fine spray of

saliva. I felt a hand on my arm. It was Anil from my class.

'She gets it . . . She'll have it tomorrow,' he said to Hayden.

'Make sure she does and tell her what'll happen if she tells,' he said, walking off.

'Are you okay?' Anil asked me when Hayden had gone.

I nodded. 'I don't . . . What does he want?' I managed.

'Payment.'

'What for?'

'For not hurting you. Remember last year when Oliver broke his arm?'

'You mean when he fell off the wall?' There'd been a big fuss about it and nobody was allowed to play on the wall any more; Oliver hadn't been too popular for a while.

'He didn't fall off the wall – it was Hayden.'

'But that's . . . How come no one knows? I mean, shouldn't we tell someone?'

'You are kidding, right?' said Anil, looking at me like I'd gone crazy. 'How come you don't know, anyhow? Everyone has to bring Hayden something every week.'

Which reminded me I didn't know what I was supposed to bring.

'Well,' said Anil, when I asked him, 'he prefers money but it has to be over fifty pence. If you can't get that then he'll make do with sweets, but if he doesn't like them you'll get a Chinese burn. Mars bars are his favourite or most things in that line. Just don't bring Jelly Babies or you'll regret it.'

That night I was so worried I couldn't sleep. Lily knew there was something wrong but I wouldn't tell her what had *happened at school. She'd stopped throwing up and told me she'd had a nice day at home with Mum and she was going to have another day off just to make sure she was better.*

That did it. I knew Hayden had said I mustn't tell anyone and I'd held out for ages, but in the end I had to tell Lily. She looked furious.

'So I have to take something tomorrow. Have you got any money?'

'I'm not giving my money to Hayden.'

'Please, Lily. If I don't have it he'll break my arm.'

Lily laughed.

'You don't understand!' I was close to tears now. 'He broke Oliver's arm because he forgot to bring something.'

'No he did not,' said Lily. 'Oliver fell off the wall because he's a clumsy idiot.'

'He didn't,' I whispered urgently. 'It was Hayden.'

Lily laughed again. How could she! Now I was crying, not only because I was scared but because Lily was being so heartless.

'Oh Milly! Don't,' said Lily. She got out of bed and climbed in beside me. 'Stop worrying,' she said, giving me a hug. 'I'll go to school with you tomorrow and it will be fine, okay?'

So Lily convinced Mum she was well enough for school and at break time we went into the playground.

'Right,' said Lily, leading me to the old loos, 'you stand here and when Hayden comes, tell him you've got something. Then I'll come out and you run away.'

I stood there while Lily disappeared round the side of the building. I felt like that goat in Jurassic Park; the one they tie up to try and lure the biggest dinosaur.

Then Hayden arrived and motioned to me to follow him round the side of the loos. As soon as he'd gone round the corner Lily appeared from the other side.

'Don't worry,' she said and followed Hayden.

I stood and waited. It could only have been about a minute but it felt like for ever. I wanted to look to check that Lily was okay, but at the same time I couldn't bring myself to look. I was just about to go and fetch someone to help when Hayden came round the side of the building. He was limping. I shrank back against the wall but he didn't even look at me.

Lily came out looking grim but perfectly unharmed.

'He won't bother you again,' she said.

'What happened?'

Lily grinned. 'I told him that, if he so much as looked at you, then I'd get Mum to put him in one of her books. I said she'd draw him as the ugliest, meanest boy in the school who everyone hated and the whole world would know it was him and it would be on the telly and everything.'

'Really? Is that what happened?'

'No,' said Lily, linking arms with me. 'It's a nice thought, though.'

I can't believe that I kissed Hayden Bailey when he was demanding money with menaces. I never did tell Lily that part. It still makes me cringe.

Chapter Nine

I couldn't get out of bed this morning. Not that I needed to because it was Sunday,; but it wasn't a nice Sunday morning feeling, like I knew I could have a long lazy lie-in. It felt more like I'd lost the use of my arms and legs. Or at least I knew they worked, it was just that the connection between my brain and my body had broken.

I didn't need to open my eyes to know that Lily wasn't there; it's a twin thing.

I couldn't even move my arm to turn on the bedside light and it's dark down here in the mornings. I could feel the weight of silence from the house above pressing down on me. I felt like I'd been buried alive in some subterranean tomb, surrounded by all my worldly possessions. One day an archaeologist would dig me up and wonder why I'd died so young. They might be confused about the significance of the doll's house, buried alongside me.

Mum poked her head round the door.

'Milly, you'd better get up. You've got a visitor.'

I shot out of bed, but Mum had gone so I couldn't ask her who it was. Who would be visiting me? For a moment I thought it might be the Americans. Perhaps they'd arrived last night and come visiting. Yeah, like that's the first thing they'd do. It was probably only Carmel, come to see how I'm getting on at the new school.

I could hear voices and laughter coming from the kitchen. Was that Effy? She'd asked for my address and phone number last week and I'd given them to her reluctantly. I hadn't expected her to call round without any warning. What if Lily had been here? I'd never hear the end of it. She wasn't going to like Effy.

It was strange seeing her in our kitchen talking to Mum, like nothing was wrong. We don't often have friends round. What am I saying? We never have friends round. The girls who like me never like Lily and the ones who like Lily get irritated with me. It's easier not to bother.

'Effy's been telling me how your new school is so different from her last one,' said Mum. I took that to mean that Effy had been relating her life story again.

'I thought we could go out, round town or something,' Effy suggested.

'That's a good idea,' said Mum. 'I'll give you some money.'

Mum went off to find her purse. I didn't really feel like going out, but it looked like I didn't have a lot of choice. We couldn't stay here and risk Lily turning up.

Like I said before, it's easy being with Effy. We went off into town and I didn't have to think because Effy organised everything. She decided which shops we'd go into and where to go for coffee. It was almost fun. It's not that she's bossy; I wanted to go to the Sunday market and she was happy to come along.

I needed some things for my hair. It's long and unruly and I wanted some more ties because I wear it in a ponytail most of the time. Effy asked me if I'd thought about having it cut. I couldn't tell her that it would be like insulting Lily, because she doesn't know about Lily and even if she did it would sound silly. Lily was talking about having hers cut a while back but she never did it. If I had mine cut it wouldn't be right.

Anyhow, I explained to Effy, if I had it cut it would have to be really short because otherwise it would just stick out all over the place because of the curls. At least if it's long the weight pulls the curls out a bit. Once, Lily and I tried to straighten our hair with some hair straighteners Lily had borrowed from a girl at school. It didn't work; it made us look like witches. Mum said there was a time in the 1980s when our hair would have been dead fashionable. That didn't help.

When we got back I didn't invite Effy in. I hope she didn't think I was being rude.

The new neighbours had arrived while I was out. I could hear them moving about upstairs. Mum said we should bake some biscuits and take them up as a welcome. I refused but

70

Mum insisted we'd have to go up and introduce ourselves tomorrow because it would be rude not to.

I lay in bed trying to hear them but it had all gone quiet. They must have gone to bed. Lily wasn't bothered.

'I don't know what all the fuss is about,' she said, turning over.

'What fuss?' I said crossly. 'Nobody's fussing.'

But then, at three o'clock in the morning, I heard someone moving about. It's nice to know that someone else is awake at that hour. I was trying to fall asleep while reading a book. I've discovered that if I read really slowly I can sometimes fall asleep without realising it. I expect the Americans have got jet lag and it's messed their body clocks up.

School's getting better. I like going now, even though the mornings are getting darker and sometimes I feel so tired I can barely function first thing. I've started drinking coffee in the morning to try and wake myself up.

The best thing about Effy is that she's good at making friends. The first few days we stuck together and had lunch by ourselves in the canteen. Then Effy said, 'Let's go and sit with them,' indicating some girls from our year. I wasn't so sure because I could see that one of them was Amy and I could tell a mile off that she's bad news. But before I could warn Effy she'd plonked herself on the end of their table and started talking to them. I kept quiet; I had a bad feeling about this. You'd have thought the girls were being friendly but I could detect an undercurrent and when they started asking Effy about her old school, St Bart's, I tried kicking Effy's

71

ankle to warn her to shut up but she just said 'Ow,' and carried on talking.

I didn't tell Effy that I wasn't happy about Amy and her friends because I didn't want to come across as paranoid but the next day, at lunchtime, I could see her looking around for them so I steered her towards a different group. I'd had a few lessons with some of them and while they were nice I'd never have dared approach them if I hadn't been so desperate to keep Effy away from Amy. That's the trouble with Effy: she's not very street-wise. She thinks everyone is as nice and uncomplicated as she is.

So we ended up with Molly, Harriet and Katy. They were really friendly but I didn't say very much because they were talking about what they'd watched on television last night and we don't have a telly to speak of. It's not like Mum's said 'no telly' or anything; it's just that the one we've got is really old and small so it's hardly worth bothering with. I had heard about most of the things they watch though so I just listened. No doubt my how to make friends book would have advised me to try and change the subject, to steer it onto something I could have joined in with, but I didn't feel ready for that.

When we were twelve Mum took us on holiday to Cornwall. We were going to visit Mum's friend Matt who used to live in the house but had moved to a commune on an organic farm. It wasn't until we were halfway down the motorway that

Mum said it wasn't exactly a holiday –, we'd be expected to help on the farm.

'What?' said Lily.

'Sorry,' said Mum, 'but it will be all hands to the deck.'

'Don't you mean, "all hands to the plough"?' I said.

Mum laughed. 'Very true,' she said, 'serves me right for using platitudes.'

'What's a platitude?' I asked. Lily gave me one of her 'don't encourage her looks'.

'It's a trite, worn-out, clichéd expression,' said Mum. 'Politicians use them all the time. See if you can think of one that's relevant to the situation.'

Mum does this all the time; tries to get us to think – especially about language.

Lily was sulking. I don't think she could think of anything.

'How about, "There's no such thing as a free lunch"?' I said.

'Very good,' said Mum. 'We can't expect to stay there and not help out. There's a big farmers' market coming up soon so there'll be plenty to do.'

'What doesn't kill you will make you stronger,' said Lily.

'Let's hope so,' said Mum.

Lily didn't like it much on the farm. She soon got bored with feeding the pigs and the chickens and hated it when we were asked to do the weeding between the rows of vegetables. There were other kids on the farm but they were all younger than us, except for Mark, who was fourteen. I liked Mark. He didn't say much to start with. I think he was shy, like me. But when he realised I was interested in the animals and liked the work, he was a lot more friendly. He didn't live in the main house where we were staying. He lived above the old stables with his mum and dad and little brother. I always tried to get the jobs where I could work with Mark and of course Lily noticed. She started teasing me. 'Mark and Milly sitting in a tree,' she'd chant if she saw me looking for him. It wasn't like that at all. I was only twelve and I didn't really fancy him, I just liked him. Maybe that's what annoyed Lily. I don't know. Maybe she did fancy him and was annoyed that he obviously preferred me.

That holiday was the first time that Lily tried to be different. I mean, look different. Up until then we'd always been proud that we were identical, but that summer Lily got one of the women living in the house to braid her hair and told me I couldn't have any in mine. It was only two thin braids at the front, done in coloured cotton with beads on the end. Mum said it looked lovely and certainly made it easier for everyone to tell us apart. I pretended not to care.

On the last day of our holiday Mark asked me if I wanted to go badger-watching with him that evening. We were in the barn, sitting on the hay because we'd run in there to escape a rain shower. Mark told me that he knew about a badger sett in the woods and if we went up there at dusk we'd get a good view of them. I love badgers and said I definitely wanted to go.

'Shall I bring Lily?' I asked Mark.

'Best not,' said Mark. 'We'll have to be quiet or we'll scare them off.'

'I might not be able to stop her from coming if she finds out about it.'

'Well, don't tell her, then. I'll meet you by the gate at half-past seven, which should give us plenty of time to get to the hide and settle in before the badgers come out.'

It was easier than I thought it would be because I didn't see much of Lily for the rest of the day. Thinking about it now I think she was avoiding me. After tea I said I'd help with putting the younger children to bed because I knew Lily hated doing that.

When I was running a bath for them Lily came into the bathroom and said, 'I've got a message for you from your precious Mark. He says make it eight o'clock,' and then she disappeared. I should have been suspicious at that point. Why didn't she ask me what was happening at eight o'clock? But I was just glad that I didn't have to explain. When I was reading the kids a story I kept looking at the clock; I was getting really excited. I'd never seen a badger in the wild. In fact, thinking about it, I'd only ever seen dead ones by the side of the road.

At eight o'clock I went to the gate but Mark wasn't there. I waited about fifteen minutes, wondering what could be holding him up, then I went to the stable block and knocked on the door. Mark's mum came to the door and I asked her if Mark was there.

'I think he's taken your sister up to the woods to look at the badgers,' she said.

I thought about going to the woods to look for them but I had no idea where the hide was and I could hardly go blundering about calling them; I'd scare the badgers for certain.

I went back to the house. I couldn't understand why Mark

had gone with Lily. Lily wasn't even interested in badgers and why had he gone without me? It wasn't until I got back to our bedroom that I began to understand. Lying coiled up on the bedside cabinet were two braids.

Lily got back two hours later. She flung herself onto the bed, laughing uncontrollably.

'You will never guess what I just did! It was the funniest thing ever,' she finally managed to say.

I didn't look up from my book but that didn't deter Lily.

'It was so funny! I went to the woods with Mark, pretending to be you!' I turned over so I had my back to her. I tried to concentrate on my book but it was impossible. I was furious. Lily could see that I wasn't enjoying her joke.

'It was easy,' she said. 'I heard you arranging it in the barn. I was in there all the time – bet you didn't know that. I heard him telling you not to tell me about it. I can't believe you listened to him. So anyhow, I just turned up at the gate at half seven and simpered a bit and didn't say much. He took me to this place in the woods where we were meant to sit quietly or something and wait for some badgers. It was dead boring so after a while I told him that I didn't care about the badgers but I'd fancied him for ages – and then I kissed him! And all the time he thought it was you!'

Chapter Ten

In the end we didn't get to meet our new neighbours until the end of the week. Mum was having a bad week, I could tell. I was pretty concerned when I took her a cup of tea one morning and saw a bottle of whisky next to the bottle of pills on her bedside cabinet. I put the tea down and she just about managed a 'thanks' before rolling over and pulling the cover over her head. I took the bottle of whisky into the kitchen. I thought about pouring it down the sink but didn't dare, so I put it in the cupboard under the sink with all the cleaning products. At least Mum would know what I thought when she saw it was gone. But then I imagined her looking for it and getting cross with me, so I took it out and put it on the draining board.

When I got home on Friday Mum was in the kitchen putting some biscuits she'd made into a tin. She insisted we go straight upstairs and give them to the Americans, but I said there was no way I was going in my school uniform so she told me to hurry up and change.

Lily was in the bedroom lounging on her bed. She was wearing her school uniform.

'We're going upstairs,' I told her.

'You might be, I'm not. I think I'll listen at the door, though.' She means the door at the top of the stairs in our hallway that leads to the house.

I didn't want to argue with her and *I* wasn't going to let Mum down by refusing to go. I thought Lily would have been dying to see the boy; she's way more into boys than I am.

We had to go outside, up the basement steps, onto the pavement and then knock on the front door. It was weird, like knocking on our own front door. I didn't like it.

A woman opened the door. She looked puzzled, then Mum introduced us and she was all smiles. She invited us in and we stood around in the hall while they made small talk and Mum handed over the biscuits. I was standing next to the new downstairs shower room and I noticed that they'd put a new shower curtain up, over the glass door. Weird. Then I remembered Lily, listening behind the basement door. Good luck to her because Mum and the woman, who had introduced herself as Mrs Wade, had moved into the kitchen.

It all sounded a bit formal. Mum didn't say she was Ms Pond, she said, 'I'm Summer and this is Milly, I wanted to say, 'It's Emily, actually,' but I didn't.

Mum and Mrs Wade had got through talking about the

flight and the move and the fact that Mr Wade had gone to the university to get settled in because he started work next week, before Mrs Wade had looked at me and said, 'Oh, I'm sorry, how rude, you must want to meet Devlin.'

I could hardly say no, so I just smiled. Mrs Wade got her phone out and sent a quick text so I assumed Devlin had gone out and she was telling him to come home. But then I heard someone coming down the stairs. The boy walked into the kitchen, still holding his phone.

'This is my son, Devlin,' said Mrs Wade.

He didn't smile, just sort of nodded our way.

'Take Milly into the lounge, Devlin,' said his mum. The boy glanced at me and turned and I had no real choice but to follow. How I wished Lily was here.

As I left the room I heard Mum telling Mrs Wade about Lily, so I shut the kitchen door behind me. If Lily was listening at the basement door like she said she would I didn't want her to hear. I kicked it as I went past, thinking it would make Lily jump. The key rattled in the lock and I suppressed the urge to unlock it and fling the door open, causing Lily to fall out onto the floor. Then I was in the front room with Devlin.

It was awkward. I couldn't think of one single thing to say that wouldn't sound stupid. Neither, it seemed, could Devlin. I sat on the sofa and tried to look like I didn't care. Devlin stood by the fireplace and really looked like he didn't care.

I wondered what Lily would do if she was here. Probably wait for him to speak. She'd probably sit and stare at him and make him feel awkward, not sit looking at everything except him, like I was doing.

I pretended to study a painting on the wall behind his head so that I could get a good look at him. I knew Lily would want a detailed description of him.

His hair was brown, like mine, but not as curly and he had a great tan. Well, he would have, coming from California. Not too bad, I thought, if he didn't look so bored. He was about a head taller than me and slim without being skinny, muscly in fact. I must have been staring, because he turned and looked straight at me and I saw for the first time that his eyes were blue. Really, really blue.

'Have you ever been to England before?' I said to cover my confusion. God! I sounded like someone out of a Jane Austen novel.

'No,' said Devlin. I waited for him to elaborate, but he didn't. Then again how could he? What else was there to say? Then I remembered the library book. It said, *Don't ask questions that have a 'yes' or 'no' answer. Ask 'leading questions' that need more than a one word answer.*

'So, what do you think of it, then? Do you like it?'

Devlin looked out of the window.

'Don't know.'

'Oh.'

'I haven't been out yet.'

'Ah.'

Why was Mum taking so long? Then, as if she knew what I was thinking, I heard them coming down the hall.

Thank God! I stood up. Mum and Mrs Wade came in.

'It's so nice that Devlin's got someone his own age to talk to,' said Mrs Wade. 'I've been trying all week to get him to go out. I was hoping that you could show him round, Milly. We're so lucky to be staying in this city, with all its history. Would you mind? How about tomorrow?'

'That would be lovely,' said Mum.

What? I glared at her, but she refused to look at me. Lily would have said she had other plans if she were here. She wouldn't have let herself be railroaded like this.

I saw Devlin glaring at his mum, but she just glared right back without blinking until he said, 'It was lovely to meet you, ma'am,' and shook Mum's hand. Then he shook mine.

'I'll be looking forward to tomorrow,' he added and I could have believed him if he'd smiled. The grown-ups seemed satisfied, though, and when the front door shut behind us Mum said, 'Americans have such lovely manners.'

When we got back downstairs Mum was in a sombre mood and I didn't want to talk about what had just happened so I got my homework out, which is code for 'Don't talk to me, I'm busy', even though it's a Friday night and nobody does homework on a Friday night.

Of course, when we were in bed Lily wanted to know all about him.

'He's got brown hair, blue eyes and he's really fit,' I told her.

'Ooh, so you fancy him, then?'

'No, I mean "fit" as in tanned and slim and muscly. Other than that he's just ordinary, nothing special.'

She wanted more details, like did he have a funny accent and did I think he fancied me?

'No,' I said and turned over, ending the conversation. I didn't want her to know that when he'd fixed his blue eyes on me I'd stopped breathing and my heartbeat had doubled in speed, or that when he'd shaken my hand the same thing had happened and I could swear that I'd felt a jolt – like an electric current had passed between us. I decided I'd been reading too many romantic novels and that Devlin had hardly even noticed me. I tried to think up a simile to describe his eyes, like they did in books. *His eyes were as warm and blue as the Aegean sea and she wanted to swim in them forever* – sort of thing. But all I could come up with was that his eyes were as blue as the cover of my English exercise book, so I gave up and got my journal out.

The summer before last, when Lily and I were thirteen, Mum decided to take us to the seaside for the holidays. At least that's what she told us, but really she wanted to go and visit an artist friend of hers who lived on the coast in Wales. There wasn't much for us to do and we took to walking to the nearest village, which had a shop and a pub and a castle. Most of the time we just sat on a wall eating ice cream and watching the tourists.

Then some boys turned up. They were local boys and after they'd driven past us a few times on their BMXs, showing off, doing wheelies and things, and looking at us out the corner of their eyes, they got a bit bolder and looked at us properly and made jokes about 'buy one get one free', which I thought was really insulting but Lily laughed anyway.

The next few times we went to the village they were always there, either messing about near us or talking to Lily. Then on the Friday of what was our last weekend in Wales they said there was a party on Saturday night and we had to come. It was going to be a barbecue on the beach; they had one every year.

It was all Lily talked about for the next twenty-four hours. I didn't want to go and spent all of the time trying to persuade Lily not to go. Mum gives us way more freedom than most girls our age get, but somehow we both knew that it was best not to mention the party to her.

Which was why, the next evening, I heard Lily telling Mum that we were going for a walk because I wanted to see if we could find any bats. This was typical of Lily. She's not stupid enough to say she wanted to go looking for bats because that would definitely have made Mum suspicious. But by saying 'Milly wants to find some bats,' in an ever so slightly 'I'm humouring her' voice, Mum didn't think anything of it. So we set off for the village and the party. There was never any question that I wouldn't go with Lily, even though I really didn't want to. For a start, if I'd refused, Lily couldn't have gone on her own because Mum would have wondered where she'd gone without me. Lily kept telling me not to be such a drag and I really tried not to be, but it didn't help that all the way there Lily kept going on about how Laura Barker had done it with Keiran Scott at Daisy's birthday party. Who cared what Laura

Barker had done? I didn't believe it anyway.

The party wasn't too bad at first. We played some frisbee on the sand with a load of other people, which was good because you don't have to talk to anyone when you're playing frisbee due to the fact that you have to stand miles apart. But then the food was ready and the boys from the village came over and sat with us. They were drinking lager and they gave me and Lily cans. I wanted to tell Lily not to drink hers, but I knew she'd never forgive me if I said it in front of them. Lily had told them we were sixteen and they seemed to believe her. I took a sip out of mine but it tasted vile so I put it on a rock and hoped no one would notice. Lily was slugging hers back and talking to Alec, which left me with Sam. The sun had gone down and it was getting cold. I made the mistake of shivering and Sam saw it as an invitation to put his arm round me. I suggested we played some more frisbee but Sam ignored me. He smelled of lager and sausages. I decided I hated Lily.

When it got dark Lily and Alec moved away. I wanted to follow them but I knew how pathetic that would look. Sam tried to put his hand up my jumper. He hadn't even tried to kiss me. I don't know much about these things but I would have thought a hand up the jumper came after a kiss. I hit his hand away and stood up. I was really panicked now; I couldn't see Lily anywhere. The light from the fire only travelled so far. Why hadn't I brought a torch? Sam gave up on me and moved away to join the others.

There were some sand dunes between the beach and the road and I decided to go and hide in them until Lily came back.

I'd just climbed the first dune when I heard voices over to the left. I froze. Then I realised that one of the voices belonged to Lily. I stood uncertainly for a while wondering what to do. I didn't want to go back to the fire where I didn't know anybody but I couldn't stand around within earshot of Lily and Alec without letting them know I was there because that would be like I was spying on them. I decided the best thing to do was to go and tell Lily that I wanted to go home.

But the voices had stopped and I had trouble locating the dip where I knew Lily and Alec must be. Which was why I nearly fell over them. They were lying in the sand and the first thing that struck me was that Lily didn't have her top on and her white bra was practically the only thing I could see in the dark. I must have accidentally kicked Alec when I came to an abrupt halt, otherwise I don't think either of them would have realised I was there because they were too preoccupied.

He broke off long enough to turn round and say something in Welsh which I was pretty sure meant that I should go away. Then Lily saw me.

'For God's sake, Milly, go away!' she hissed.

'Yeah,' said Alec. 'Either go away or come and join in.'

Lily laughed. I clenched my fists. I was trembling. I wanted to turn and run but I couldn't.

'You do know she's only thirteen?' My voice came out way louder than I'd intended.

Alec sat up. 'You said you were sixteen.'

'I am,' said Lily. 'She's lying.'

'I'm not. I should know, she's my twin sister and I'm only

thirteen. You could end up with a sex offender's record.'

Alec swore and stood up. Lily grabbed his trouser leg. 'Come on,' she said to him, 'just ignore her and she'll go away.'

'Forget it!' said Alec and he stormed away into the darkness.

Lily grabbed her top and pulled it back on. I didn't need to see her face to know that she was furious.

'God, Milly! You're such a retard!' and that was the last thing she said to me for three whole days.

Chapter Eleven

Early on Saturday morning I sat at the top of the stairs listening in to Devlin and his mum. I had to climb over a load of stuff to get up there. When Jeanie locked the door at the top, Mum started to use the stairs to store things on, like a set of giant shelves. There were books stacked up the side, a basket of washing, a heap of files and letters and some random objects like a cheese grater, a packet of fly papers and a clock which was waiting for a new battery. Anyhow, I managed to clear a path and I settled on the top stair with my ear pressed to the door.

'Are you going to go to the basketball club?' That was Mrs Wade.

'I don't know. I haven't decided yet. Basketball's not really my thing, you know that. Why can't there be a baseball club?'

'I know, honey, I'm sorry.' There was a short pause.

'You could always try something new: soccer or cricket or rugby, even.'

'Rugby?'

'It's sort of like football, except here they call soccer "football". I don't know. When we've got Sky Sports installed you could watch the television and find out.'

The reason I was listening in to the conversation was that *How to Make Friends* said, *Find out what the other person likes and strike up a conversation on that subject.* So I thought this would be a good shortcut to finding out what interested Devlin because he wasn't exactly the most talkative person. Now I knew he was into baseball, but that was no good because I knew nothing about baseball except it's a bit like rounders and you wear a big glove.

'What are you doing?' Lily was peering up at me through the banisters.

I made mad, shushing mimes at her.

'You total perv. You're stalking the new boy!'

'I am not,' I hissed at her.

'You are too. You're not in love with him, are you? Please tell me you haven't got a gigantic crush on him.'

'You're a fine one to talk. You were doing this last night!'

'That was different.'

'Go away!'

'Weirdo,' said Lily, but she went away. She'd already dismissed Devlin as a loser, which was fine by me because he's going to be my friend – not hers.

I held my breath and kept listening, terrified that they'd heard me but I needn't have worried. They were in the sitting room, though, so I could hear them clearly enough.

'I thought if you joined some sort of sports club you might make some friends. You're not going to meet anyone shut up in the house all the time,' Devlin's mum said.

Except ME, I wanted to shout through the door.

'What's the point?' said Devlin. 'It's not like I'm ever going to see them again once we go back home.'

'You never know,' said his mum. 'I met my best friend Helen at summer camp. We didn't see each other again for twenty years but we kept writing during all that time.'

Mrs Wade's voice was suddenly louder. She was in the corridor right outside the basement door. I held my breath. 'Don't be long,' she was saying, 'the girl from downstairs will be here soon. I'll be in the kitchen,' and I could hear her little kitten heels going off into the distance.

When I got back to the bedroom Lily was lying on her bed.

'So, what did you find out about lover boy then?'

'Don't call him that! Nothing much – except that he's missing playing baseball. I didn't have him down as the sporty type.' Although I suppose that was why he was so muscly.

'No, he's more the "stay home and bake some cookies with Mother" type.'

'Don't be mean. How would you like it if you had to go and live in a strange place?'

Lily didn't say anything to that, though her injured silence spoke volumes.

But being Lily meant that the silence didn't last long.

'I reckon he's gay,' she said. 'You're wasting your time.'

'Of course he's not gay!'

Lily just smiled. 'I'm not coming with you.'

'You weren't invited.'

'You'll be on your own – with a boy.' I knew she was trying to wind me up so I didn't reply.

'Don't go pretending I'm there. You know, in your head.' How did she know that's what I do? I hate her for knowing that.

I know I'm getting better at being Emily though. On the walk to the bus stop in the mornings I don't pretend Lily's with me any more. Instead I use the time to change into Emily. By the time I get on the bus and start talking to Effy I'm a normal person. Emily Pond, going to school with her new friend.

I knocked on the front door upstairs and Mrs Wade answered it. I really wished she'd tell me her first name because Mrs Wade is a bit of a mouthful. Maybe it's an American thing, calling adults by their surname.

I'd got butterflies in my stomach, I don't know why. I was only showing someone round town, how hard could it be? There was no sign of Devlin, though, and Mrs Wade looked a bit nervous as she ushered me into the front room.

'Milly,' she said, 'your mum told me about what happened to you – you know – recently.' She fiddled with the zip on her cardigan. I don't know who was more embarrassed, her or me. 'Anyway, the thing is, I'd rather you didn't talk to Devlin about it, if you don't mind. It's just that he's . . .' and then Devlin walked in and she shut up.

Devlin looked angry, like he knew she'd been talking about him. I know I must have looked angry as well. How dare she? I wasn't going to tell Devlin about it, but that was my choice. How dare she tell me what I could and could not say about anything?

So we both left the house in a temper and marched down the street in silence. Now his mum had told me not to mention anything about what had happened, it was all I could think about and I felt like I was about to blurt it all out, just because she'd told me not to.

'Where are we going?' asked Devlin, sounding almost as miserable as I felt.

I snapped out of my own self-pity and said, 'We'll cross the bridge and go into town.'

I glanced at him. He didn't look happy; he had his shoulders hunched and his hands in his pockets. He looked like he'd rather be anywhere but here with me.

'What are you into?' I asked him. 'Romans or Jane Austen?'

Devlin looked completely blank. He obviously hadn't done any research before he came here.

'They're the two main things this city is famous for,' I

explained. 'Unless you'd rather go shopping.'

'I don't know much about the Romans,' said Devlin, like he was really making an effort. 'Mum's into Jane Austen.'

'Well, the Romans invaded us in AD43, or some time around then, and they came here because there were hot springs and they built some baths around them. I suppose they must have found it cold after Italy.'

Actually I know loads about the Romans and about the pagans who were here before them, but I didn't go on about them in case I sounded like a tour guide. Besides, I didn't want Devlin to think I was some kind of history geek.

'Where's this bridge then?' said Devlin.

'Bridge?'

'You said we were going across a bridge.'

'Oh!' I said. 'We just crossed it. You wouldn't know because it's got shops built on it.'

'Right,' said Devlin.

'I could show you, if you like. From the other side, above the river.'

'No, don't bother.'

This was going to be even harder than I thought. We carried on up Bridge Street and I thought it would be all right when we got to the Baths, because you can't visit Bath without visiting the Baths, that would be mental. But I was wrong. We went in to pay; it's not cheap but Mum had given me loads of money so I could show Devlin all the sights. Devlin was looking around and he'd picked up a leaflet about the Baths. It had photos of the main pool in it and I wanted to snatch it off him because I thought he was spoiling the surprise.

'Is this it?' he said.

'That's part of it,' I told him. 'There's loads of other stuff. Come on, I'll show you.'

'I've changed my mind,' said Devlin. 'I don't want to go in.'

'What? But I thought . . .'

'I don't want to go in there, okay.'

What the hell? We fought our way out. There was a whole bunch of French school kids queuing up outside. Mum says there used to be a tourist season and, when she first came here, the summer and the spring were the times when the town was full of tourists. Now it's full of them all the time. And a lot of them are American. And I was stuck with the most reluctant one in the world. Who wouldn't want to see the Baths?

So then I began to wonder what to do with him. I didn't want to suggest the Abbey, because that seemed like the most boring thing and he didn't look like a religious type of person. The Pump Rooms were right next to us but there's not much to see in them. I could insist he tried 'taking the waters'. That would serve him right, because they taste foul and the last time I tried them I nearly puked. I was pretty sure he wouldn't appreciate the Fashion Museum or the Jane Austen Centre, or the art galleries. I was trying to think of something more exciting.

All the time that I was wondering what to do next, Devlin

was just standing there next to me. I started to walk, just to make it look like I had a plan in mind. Devlin was looking at the shops as we went past but he didn't seem to want to go into any of them. We ended up near the river and I had a brainwave.

'I know, let's go on a river cruise, then you can see the city from there.'

You can get a boat from the weir. We were approaching Grand Parade where you can lean on the stone balustrade and look down on the river and the weir. The weir is sort of crescent-shaped but like a crescent that someone's squeezed inwards so it's long and thin. There are three steps that the river cascades over and I love looking at it. I could sit all day just looking at it.

Devlin followed me to the balustrade but didn't lean over it like I was doing. I pointed out the boat which was moored in the calm water beside the weir.

'So what do you think? Do you fancy a river trip?'

'No thanks,' Devlin said. I noticed that his eyes had turned a shade darker.

'Oh go on, it'll be fun,' I told him.

Devlin didn't reply. He just turned his back on the river. This was hopeless. How could I show someone around when they didn't want to do anything? Then I thought, what if it's just that he doesn't want to do it with me? I wondered about going home and leaving him to get on with it on his own. I bet that's what Lily would have done. Mum would be furious, though. She'd say it was a really rude thing to do, even if I explained that it was Devlin who was rude by being so uncooperative and unfriendly.

Maybe I'd been suggesting the wrong things. If Devlin was into sport I should be thinking along those lines. Trouble is, I don't do much sport myself and the only thing I could think of was the Thermae Spa Bath. I'd been there a few times with Mum and Lily and loved it.

The swimming pool is warm because it's fed from the thermal springs, but the best thing about it is that it's built on the rooftop so you can swim around looking down on the Abbey and the rest of the city. I thought about what it would be like to go there with Devlin. If I was honest I didn't much fancy swimming myself but I'd do it if I had to, so I explained about the pool to Devlin and asked him if he wanted to go.

He just shook his head and gave me a really dark look like he couldn't even be bothered to talk to me any more.

I was practically in tears; tears of frustration and embarrassment. What was his problem? I couldn't believe I ever wanted to be friends with him. Perhaps he thought I fancied him and he wanted to make it clear that the feeling wasn't mutual and that's why he was being so unfriendly. Well, I'd show him that I didn't fancy him, or even like him.

A tour bus had just pulled in at the bus stop at the end of the parade. I didn't bother asking Devlin if he wanted to go on it. I just grabbed his sleeve and pulled him on. It was an open-topped bus and I marched upstairs with Devlin following behind. I stood back and wordlessly offered him the window seat, or what would have been if there had been any windows. When he'd sat down I took the seat behind him. I didn't care if I was being rude, I was fed up. Let the tour guide tell him about the city; I'd had enough.

So for the next hour the bus trundled around the sights and I sat staring at the back of Devlin's head, wondering what was going on inside of it. He just sat looking ahead all the time like he wasn't interested in anything, which made me cross because I like my home town and he could at least have made an effort. Mind you, he did look a bit more relaxed than he had earlier and I could only conclude that it was because I wasn't sitting next to him.

When the bus pulled up in the Orange Grove, which is where we'd started, we got off and headed for Pulteney Bridge and home. We hadn't spoken to each other since before we'd got on the bus, which made it very hard to break the silence. We walked along Grand Parade but not on the side that overlooks the river, which meant that we had to cross the road at the end by the Art Gallery. We were waiting for the lights to change, even though there wasn't masses of traffic around, when a man came running up the street. Now, normally there's nothing very odd about a man running up the street, but this particular man was wearing a wedding dress. A full, white, frothy wedding dress which he was holding up above his knees so he could run faster. He had hairy legs, short hair and a beard, and for a moment I wondered for some obscure reason if it was my dad.

I decided to play it really cool and pretend that there was nothing unusual about a man running up the street wearing a wedding dress. I mean, Devlin comes from Los Angeles and stuff like that probably happens there all the time.

The man had ran straight past us and carried on up Bridge Street. I half turned to watch him, because I couldn't help myself, and that's when I caught Devlin's eye and we started laughing. It was weird seeing Devlin laugh. Weird but nice.

Anyhow, the man in the wedding dress had certainly broken the ice because we spent the next few minutes speculating about him, but neither of us could come up with a good explanation as to why he was wearing a wedding dress or why he was running.

By this time we'd crossed the bridge, and because we were talking to each other and I didn't want the whole day to have been a disaster, I suggested we go for a coffee as we were about to pass my favourite café. I regretted it as soon as I'd said it because I thought Devlin was going to say, 'No thanks,' again, like he had to everything else. But he didn't, he said, 'Yeah, why not?', so I led him down some steps which come out above the river on the other side from the Parade. There's a little café halfway down where you can get a drink and have it overlooking the river and the weir.

Because the café is so small you can hardly ever get a seat inside and besides, I like looking over the railings. I thought everything was going fine until we got down to the café and I looked back to ask Devlin what he wanted.

I could tell immediately, from the look on his face, that he'd closed down again.

What had I done? He'd said he wanted a coffee and now he was being all weird again. For a brief moment he'd been fine, actually fun for about five minutes while we were discussing the wedding-dress thing.

Just as I got to the front of the queue one of the small tables inside the café became free. Devlin scooted over to it and sat down. I wanted to sit outside but Devlin looked rooted to the spot, so I bought the coffees and took them over.

The drinks weren't too hot, which was a relief because I think we were both desperate to finish them and go. I didn't know why I'd thought this would be a good idea. The funny, friendly Devlin had disappeared.

I tried talking to him but he was strangely preoccupied; all silent and brooding. It occurred to me that he might have a girlfriend back home and he was feeling guilty about having coffee with me. I wanted to ask him but I didn't have the nerve. I stirred my coffee and decided I needed to get a grip. What did it matter if Devlin didn't like me?

When we left he started walking really fast and I had to practically run to keep up with him. He was obviously desperate to get home and away from me.

We said goodbye and he went in through the front door and I went down the basement steps, which felt weird because we were going into the same house.

I used to fancy a boy at school. His name was Ben and I couldn't stop thinking about him. I never told anyone how much I fancied him, not even Lily. He was in the year above us, so I only ever saw him in assembly or during break and lunchtimes or on the bus. He didn't get on our bus but that was the best time, because I could sit on the bus pretending to gaze out of the window, when really I was looking at him while he waited at the bus stop.

Lily was always telling me which boys she fancied and she'd even been out with some of them, but I never told her about Ben. He was my secret. He was special and I didn't want to ruin it by talking about him. I daydreamed all the time about meeting up with him, maybe in the park or bumping into him in town and walking round together, and how he'd hold my hand or put his arm round me or buy me a bracelet that I could wear all the time to remind me of him.

Writing about it now makes it sound pathetic but it wasn't.

But then one night, when we were doing our homework, Lily said, 'Have you seen that boy in year ten? Ben. He's drop-dead gorgeous.'

I pretended I didn't know who she was talking about, but my heart and my brain were in turmoil.

Was she winding me up? Did she somehow know? And why was she calling him 'drop-dead gorgeous'? Lily didn't normally say things like that; she was more likely to say she wouldn't mind a piece of him or something more crude. I sensed a trap.

'So you're not interested in him, then?' she asked.

'I might be – if I knew who you meant,' I said in what I hoped was a bored-sounding voice.

She let it drop and we carried on with our homework. I was more careful after that. I stopped gazing at him out of the bus window; I sat on the other side and I mentioned a few other boys to put her off the scent.

But about a month after that the worst thing happened. I was eating my lunch when I looked up and saw Lily talking to him. They were too far away for me to hear what was being said but I didn't need to. Everything about Lily made it obvious. She was standing quite close to him and looking up at him through her eyelashes. God! And she was twisting a strand of hair round and round her finger at the same time. Pathetic! She looked like some idiot heroine out of a gushy romance film.

I couldn't eat any more of my lunch and I didn't talk to her for the rest of the day, but she didn't seem to notice. When I got on the bus I couldn't stop myself from sitting on the pavement side to get a look at him. Then I wished I hadn't because Lily was there, talking to him again. She nearly missed the bus, but she jumped on at the last minute and flung herself into the seat next to me looking so smug I could have slapped her.

I turned my back on her and as the bus pulled away I caught a glimpse of Ben, and I'm pretty sure I wasn't imagining it but I thought he looked ecstatic.

Lily kept that smug look all the way home until we got indoors, then she said, 'You know that boy you've fancied for ever? Well, I've only gone and got you a date with him!'

I must have been standing with my mouth open, gaping moronically.

'Don't look so horrified, it was easy. I think he must have fancied you for ages.'

'What do you mean?'

'Well, you know you've been mooning over him and everything? I knew you'd never do anything about it so I thought I'd help you out. I was talking to him . . .'

'You mean flirting with him!' I practically yelled. Lily looked hurt.

'Well, yes . . . I was. But it's all right because he thought he was talking to you.'

'And how, exactly, does that make it all right?'

'Don't you see?' said Lily. 'He asked me out . . . at the bus stop; which means he was asking you out because he thought I was you. I told him I was Milly and I made my skirt look longer and I was really nice . . .'

'You weren't being like me! I wouldn't have flirted with him!'

'No, and you'd never have got anywhere. I've got you a date and you've got about an hour to get ready,' she said, looking at the clock. 'Then you're to meet him in front of the cathedral.'

What! I couldn't believe it. My head was spinning.

Things deteriorated pretty fast after that. Lily couldn't understand why I wasn't pleased and I couldn't get through to her that it was none of her business and she'd ruined everything.

'God, Milly. I thought I was doing you a favour. Why can't you just be glad and go on the date! What is your problem?'

I couldn't tell her because I didn't know. All I knew was that I'd been perfectly happy before and now I wasn't.

'You go on the date, then!' I screamed at her. 'Seeing as you're so keen on him.'

Lily looked crestfallen. 'I'm sorry, I thought it was what you wanted. I was just trying to help.'

101

'Well you haven't and I'm not going!'

'You can't leave him standing there,' said Lily, 'It's not fair. You'll have to go.'

'I don't have to. You made the date – you go!'

Why didn't I go on that date? It was what I'd been dreaming about for so long. Maybe that was the problem; maybe I knew that in my daydreams everything was perfect and I was scared that the reality wouldn't match up to the fantasy. Or maybe I was just plain scared. Scared of meeting up with a boy, scared of making a fool of myself and scared of disappointing him because I was me and not Lily.

I went into the bedroom, lay on the bed and turned my face to the wall. I heard Lily come in and get ready to go out, then I felt her sit on the side of my bed.

'Please go.'

I ignored her and she sighed.

'I'm going now. I'll let him down gently,' said Lily, 'but I can't live your life for you, Milly.' And she was gone.

Huh. She'd done a pretty good job of it so far, I thought.

I don't know what she said to Ben because I never asked her and she didn't tell me; she just carried on afterwards like nothing had ever happened between us.

But she was right. Only I can live my life – especially now, after what happened.

I think I'm ready to write about it now.

Chapter Twelve

Lily wasn't around when I got in. I went into the bedroom and opened the front of the doll's house. I hadn't replaced Jeanie and David with Mr and Mrs Wade and Devlin and it was bothering me.

I got the shoebox out from under the bed and picked out three random dolls. I didn't care any more which ones I used, I just wanted to make up the numbers. Then I spotted a small plastic model of Eeyore on the windowsill. Perfect. I was going to use that for Devlin; it would serve him right for being such a grump.

There was a part of me that didn't want to bother with this stupid ritual any more. Up until recently it had been a good way of keeping track of who was living in the house, which seemed pointless now. Devlin obviously didn't want anything to do with us.

Before I put the new dolls in and there was just us downstairs, it hit me as to exactly how small my family had become. Not for the first time I began to wonder about grandparents. I'd got used to not knowing who my dad was and accepted the fact that I'd never know. His parents were never going to be grandparents to us, but Mum's parents had to be somewhere. Before, whenever we'd asked about them, Mum always shrugged off our questions and said it wasn't important. Well, she was wrong. It had suddenly become very important. What if something happened to Mum?

I found her in the sitting room reading a book. She looked up when I came in and I said, 'Mum, I want to talk to you.' She put her book down.

'What is it?'

'I want to know about your mum and dad. I mean, they're my grandparents and I've never met them. I don't know anything about them and I think I have a right to know.'

Mum looked through me for a whole minute, like she was thinking really hard. Eventually she said, 'They're called Eileen and Frank Pond and they live in Wimbledon.'

I couldn't believe it. It was that easy.

'So how come I've never met them?'

Mum sighed. 'It's complicated.'

'How do you mean?' It didn't sound very complicated to me.

'The thing is, when I got pregnant they didn't approve

because I wasn't married. We argued. Milly, shut your mouth, it's hanging open.' I closed my mouth.

'I know what you're going to say,' Mum continued. 'This is the twenty-first century and all that, but you have to understand that they're from a different generation. Actually, they're quite old. I was adopted, which was something they didn't tell me until I got pregnant and then it all came out.'

Mum looked cross, like she was remembering the awful scene and I felt guilty for reminding her about it.

'Anyway, things were said, hurtful things, and we haven't really been in touch since.'

'Okay, sorry,' I said and went back to my room.

I brought it up with Ted on my next visit.

'So what's the problem?' he said.

'I don't know. It's not like I've lost anything. I've never had grandparents, and I still don't have any. But I sort of thought they were dead or something and then I found out they weren't, they were living in Wimbledon, and just for a second I thought perhaps I could go and see them.'

'Would your mum mind if you contacted them?'

'I don't know. Probably, you know what she's like; stubborn as hell. Besides, what if I got in touch with them and then I didn't like them? It would be embarrassing. I think it's best if I just forget about the whole thing.'

'How's the journal going?' asked Ted.

'I'm working on it,' I told him. Ted asking made me feel

prickly and I wondered if that's how Mum feels when people ask her how her next book's going.

I sort of want to write about what happened, but at the same time it scares me. I'm going to try though. I might start on it tonight.

Lily and I were in the kitchen, trying to scrape together a picnic.

Lily had woken up early and shaken me until I woke up too, and told me we were going on an adventure.

It's true it was unseasonably cold that day, Sunday, April 20th. Lily was unstoppable though and pulled all the covers off my bed to prevent me from snuggling back down to sleep. Sunday was a lie-in day and I reluctantly got dressed. She wouldn't tell me where we were going, it was a surprise.

I think she was hoping that we'd be able to sneak out before anyone else woke up and asked where we were going. But the sun was out and when we got to the kitchen Jeanie was in the backyard, hanging out some sheets on the line.

We made it into a game – trying to find a picnic without her seeing us, though I was sure she could hear us giggling a mile off. We knew better than to try and find a picnic in our own kitchen where the bread was always brown and grainy and there was nothing like crisps or biscuits.

As it turned out we didn't have much more luck upstairs. We managed to find two boiled eggs and the tail-end of a loaf of white bread, but we couldn't be bothered to make them into sandwiches so we stuffed them into a carrier bag, along with a bottle of salad cream and an apple and a dry-looking satsuma that had, not unsurprisingly, been overlooked in the bottom of the fruit bowl.

We were just casting about the kitchen, trying to find any loose change that might have been left lying around because, Lily said, we'd have to go some of the way on the bus, when Archie walked in.

'What are you doing? Where are you going? I want to come.'

I cringed. Archie really brought out the worst in Lily and I suspect Lily brought out the worst in Archie, too.

'Go away, Squit,' she said in her bored voice. We used to call him Squib because he was on the small side for seven, but then Lily had changed it to 'Squit' one day because he'd had a tummy upset. I went back to calling him Archie when she did that. I felt sorry for him because Lily was always so mean to him.

'You can't come with us because we haven't got enough food for three,' Lily told him. She was whispering because she didn't want to alert Jeanie to what we were doing. There are two Lilys: the charming, cheerful one that she wants the adults to see and the cruel, dismissive one that comes out when people like Archie are around.

Archie left the kitchen and we could hear him thudding up the stairs. Lily thought she'd won so we started to get our outdoor things on.

'I think we'd better wear our wellies,' Lily decided, but I couldn't find mine.

'I think they're in Mum's room,' I told her after we'd looked everywhere else.

'We can't go in there,' said Lily. 'She'll wake up and want to come with us.'

I found a rucksack, though, so I stuffed the lunch bag into it. 'Should we take a phone?' I asked.

'You can if you want. Mine hasn't got any credit on it,' Lily replied.

'Mine needs recharging,' I said.

Lily was putting on David's old duffle coat.

'What do you want to wear that smelly thing for?' I said.

'Because it's cold. Anyhow, it's dead retro.'

'It makes you look like Paddington Bear,' I told her.

Then Archie came thumping back down the stairs. He was clutching a banana, a yoghurt and a teaspoon, and a packet of chocolate biscuits. 'I've got my picnic,' he announced and started to pull his shoes on. I glanced at Lily. This was the first time that we realised the others were keeping food in their rooms and not in the kitchen where we could get it.

'You still can't come,' Lily told him. 'We've only got enough bus fare for two.'

'I've got my own,' said Archie, waving a five-pound note at us. I could tell Lily was wavering at the sight of all that money but she held firm.

'You can't stop me coming,' Archie announced. 'You can't stop me walking down the road and getting on a bus and then getting off the bus and then . . .' He had to stop because he didn't know what was going to happen or where we were going.

Lily was getting impatient. She wanted to go and we all knew this argument could go on for ages and then result in him following us and ruining the adventure.

So she played her trump card. 'Milly – you decide.'

I stared at her. She was so certain I was going to side with her. I stared at Archie. I knew that if I told him he couldn't come he'd back down. But I couldn't do it; I just stood looking at each of them in turn and saying nothing.

In my mind this moment lasts for ever, though it can only really have been a few seconds. This is the moment that I play over and over again in my mind and sometimes I hear myself saying, 'No, sorry, Archie, you can't come,' and watch him as he thumps away up the stairs. If only that was what had happened.

But I didn't. I did nothing. It amazes me how doing nothing resulted in such dire consequences.

So I said nothing and Lily finally lost patience and said, 'Well, I'm going anyway,' and grabbed her duffle coat and went out the door. I followed her and Archie followed me and that's how we arrived at the bus stop: a sad little line following Lily on her adventure.

We got on the first bus that came along. I'm sure Lily didn't know where we were going, she was just making it up as we went along. Maybe that was the adventure.

Archie seemed to know that he was there on sufferance so he sat quietly and didn't make a nuisance of himself.

The bus drove out into the countryside and I wondered where Lily was going to get off, or if she even knew and how she would decide. I looked out the window at the trees and cows and houses. The bus stopped in a village and three boys got on. They were older than us and they came up the stairs where we were sitting. Lily was immediately on high alert. She followed them with her eyes as they made their way to the back of the bus.

Lily kept turning round to look at them so I kicked her on the shin.

'Stop it! They're not interested in us, for God's sake,' I told her. 'And even if they were, I'm not interested in them.'

'Well, I might be,' said Lily. 'The one in the blue hoodie isn't bad.'

I decided to ignore her and them. But when we got to the next village and the boys got up to get off the bus, Lily watched them disappear down the stairs then stood up and said, 'Come on, we're getting off here too.' It was so obvious she was following them and I really didn't want to, but Lily was already halfway down the stairs, so I followed her and Archie followed me.

Chapter Thirteen

I knew that Amy was trouble. She turned up in our religious studies class today. It turns out she was meant to be there all along but had been sent to the 'out time' room for a month for bad behaviour. If it was meant to reform her it didn't work.

When we walked into the room Amy said in a loud, posh voice, 'I used to go to St *Fart's*, don't you know, darling!' which isn't how Effy speaks but we got the point. Naturally we ignored her but I could see that Effy was embarrassed and upset. Luckily the teacher arrived and told us to get our work out which we did, apart from Amy who got her nail varnish out instead.

When the teacher told her to get her books out Amy said, 'Who's going to make me?'

The teacher ignored this remark and got some paper out

of the drawer and put it on Amy's desk in front of her. Amy made a big show of 'accidentally' knocking it onto the floor.

The teacher went back to her desk and got a report card out and started filling it in. Anyone who's been on out time has to go a whole week without a behaviour mark. Amy wasn't going to make it through the day.

Mrs Clark, our religious studies teacher, is okay. Katy told me she's covering for their other teacher who's on maternity leave. When she'd filled in the card I thought she was going to give it to Amy and tell her to take it to the office but she put it back in the drawer.

She then told us about the new project she wanted us to do. We have to write about the worst day of our lives and then put a positive spin on it. She said it cheerfully, as if she couldn't imagine us having anything really bad to write about.

I wondered if Mrs Clark had really thought this project through. Asking a room full of adolescent girls to write about the worst day of their lives was a bit risky if you ask me. It could open up a whole can of worms.

Amy started acting up again and Mrs Clark was forced to deal with her.

Most people were chatting among themselves, trying to work out exactly which day was the worst. I could hear one girl telling her friend that it must have been last Christmas Day when her mum gave her a pair of boots and a new handbag, and how pleased she was, and then she found out they were fakes and she spent the rest of the day in tears.

Mrs Clark must have decided she'd had enough of Amy because she got the report card out of the desk drawer and handed it to her, telling her to go and report to Mr Hargreaves. I'd die of fright if I had to report to Mr Hargreaves. He's seriously scary, which is probably why he was chosen to deal with the trouble-makers. Amy took the card and held it up in front of Mrs Clark, then calmly tore it in half and dropped the bits in the bin. Mrs Clark pressed a button on her mobile phone. She must have Mr Hargreaves on speed dial. She asked him to come to room twenty-four and pick up Amy.

I glanced round at the other girls. They all looked either bored or annoyed, except Effy who looked shocked.

'You must have had girls like that at your old school. There's always one,' I said.

Effy swallowed. 'No, not that bad,' she said. 'There were girls who were mean and stuff, but if they'd behaved like that,' she nodded in Amy's direction, 'they would have been "asked to leave".'

At lunch we sat with Katy, Harriet and Molly again. They were talking about the project and they asked us what we were going to write about.

'I suppose it would have to be when my dad went bust and told me he couldn't afford to send me to St Bart's any more,' said Effy. 'Of course the positive spin on that is you guys,' she said, looking round at us all. 'I'd never have met you if I'd stayed at my old school.'

There was a silence after that and I wondered if Effy had

embarrassed the others, but when I looked up I realised they were all staring at me expectantly.

'Come on, Emily,' said Molly.

'Yeah, what was your worst day ever?' said Harriet.

I swallowed. The piece of sandwich I was eating wouldn't go down. I was sure I'd gone red with the effort of holding back my tears. What if I told them? What if I came right out with it now? Just said it. Told them about Sunday, April 20th.

'I don't think Emily's decided yet,' said Effy. The look she gave me showed me she knew there was a problem and she changed the subject. 'So, what do you lot do at the weekends? Do you want to meet up with us in town on Saturday?'

I gave myself a mental shake and tried to concentrate on being Emily, having lunch with her friends and planning the weekend. Which reminded me of last weekend and the disastrous trip out with Devlin. If it wasn't for Sunday, April 20th, last Saturday would be way up there on the list of worst days.

And then, just so that I could join in with the conversation, I told them about Devlin. Not the disastrous day out, that was kind of embarrassing, but about the fact that an American boy had moved in upstairs.

I never expected the reaction I got. They went wild. It was like I'd said Justin Bieber had moved in upstairs or something.

'Oh my God, is he really good-looking?' said Molly, and before I could answer Katy said, 'How old is he? Has he got a girlfriend?' and Harriet, who was bobbing up and down in her seat said, 'We've got to meet him! Invite us all round . . . No! I know, have a party!'

'Oooh yes, a party!' said Molly and Katy together.

I couldn't help laughing. Yeah, right. A party with five girls and Devlin. He'd love me for that. Especially as three of the girls were practically drooling at the thought of him.

'He's just a boy,' I said. 'He's pretty ordinary-looking really and I think he's a bit shy.' I was tempted to tell them he was also rude and uncooperative and downright unfriendly, but I didn't because I thought it might be just me that he didn't like. In fact, if I introduced him to some other people, I'd be able to tell if it was just me that he was unfriendly towards. The trouble is I couldn't have a party; I couldn't have people over to the flat. Not with Mum the way she was at the moment . . . and I hadn't told them about Lily and I wanted to keep it that way.

'I know,' said Effy, 'bring him into town on Saturday and take him to the Posh Nosh café and we'll all be in there and you can introduce us to him.'

'Yeah, good idea,' said Molly.

I wasn't so sure. For a start, how was I going to get him to come out again when he'd made it so plain last time that he was not enjoying himself?

But I didn't want to tell them it was never going to happen and I wanted to go out with them on Saturday even if he didn't.

'Okay,' I said, 'I'll see if I can get him to come and I'll meet you all in there at eleven o'clock.'

I'd just go on my own and tell them he was busy and couldn't make it. There was no way I was going to ask him along.

'You haven't told us what he looks like,' said Molly. 'Does he look like Zac Efron?'

I must have looked completely blank. I hadn't got a clue who they were talking about.

'You know,' said Harriet, 'Troy from *High School Musical*? You must have seen *High School Musical*!'

'Um . . . no,' I said.

'Okay,' said Kate, 'does he look like Taylor Lautner or Robert Pattinson?'

'You must know who they are,' said Harriet. 'You have seen *Twilight*, haven't you?'

'I've read it,' I said, relieved.

'Oh my God,' said Molly. 'Have you seen anything? Please tell me you've seen *Mean Girls*. It's my favourite film ever!'

I had to admit I'd never seen *Mean Girls*. Or *Confessions of a Teenage Drama Queen* or *10 Things I Hate About You*, which were all, apparently, classics which I absolutely had to see.

'Right, that's it,' said Katy. 'The girl needs educating. How about you all come round to mine on Saturday, after the café, and we'll have a film night? You can all stay over if you want.'

I did want. I wanted to very much but I couldn't. Not for the night. Not with Mum . . . well, not just now. I knew if

I asked her she'd say yes, she'd be pleased for me, but I just couldn't. Not yet.

'I'd love to,' I said, 'but I can't . . . not for the night.'

'Tell you what,' said Effy, 'we'll come, but I'll get my dad to pick us up late.'

The others looked disappointed but they didn't argue. I was secretly pleased that Effy wasn't going to stay over. I didn't want to feel like the odd one out.

And all the time they were chatting and all through the rest of the day there was a little voice in the back of my mind going, 'The worst day, the worst day, tell them about your worst day ever.' I thought about my journal and how I had started to write about it and suddenly I wanted to get home and finish it. Could I stop going to Ted's if I managed to write about what happened? Perhaps I could ask him next time I went. But would that seem rude? It might sound like I hated going there and would do anything to get out of it. I was sure he'd understand though. He'd know it was because I'd had enough and I just wanted to be normal again.

The bus pulled away. Lily, Archie and I stood on the pavement next to the bus stop. Lily was watching the boys as they walked down the street.

'What now?' I said.

One of the boys, the one in the blue hoodie, turned round and looked at us. Lily smiled at him so I poked her in the ribs with my elbow. Why did she have to be so obvious?

I looked around. The side of the street where we were standing had houses dotted along it and I could see a pub halfway down. It was called The Badger and Stoat. For a moment it made me think of Mark in Cornwall and how Lily had tricked him. There was a sign outside the pub with a painting of a badger on it and a stoat winding between its feet. If we were animals, I thought, I would be a badger and Lily would be a stoat.

Across the road was a long stone wall, about a metre high. On the other side of the wall was a wood. The trees were covered in the first, bright green leaves of spring. Opposite the bus stop where we were still standing was an old, rusty iron gate. Someone had made a sign and hung it on one of the bars with wire. The white paint had gone green, but the lettering was still visible.

It said No Admittance.

The boys had nearly reached the pub. For one awful moment I thought Lily was planning to follow them in there. But she crossed the road and slung her leg over the rusty gate.

'Come on,' she shouted over her shoulder at us, as she climbed over. Archie and I crossed the road.

'Lily, we can't go in there, it says so,' I told her, pointing to the sign.

'Well I'm going,' said Lily, crunching her way into the trees. Archie started to climb the gate. I glanced down the road towards the pub. The three boys had stopped outside the pub door. They were watching us. The boy in the blue hoodie was talking to his mates and pointing in our direction. He had

taken a few steps towards us and it looked like he was trying to persuade the other two to follow him.

Archie had reached the other side and stood there waiting for me. I quickly climbed over, grabbed Archie's hand and dived into the trees. I didn't know if we were being followed or not. My heart was racing by the time we caught up with Lily and I suspected it was fear rather than exertion that was causing it to beat so fast.

'I'm hungry,' said Archie.

I saw Lily looking around for somewhere to sit so we could eat our picnic. I was listening hard to see if I could hear the boys coming through the woods after us.

'Let's have it later,' I said, leading them further into the woods.

There was a sort of path that we were following but it had been blocked by a huge tree. The tree had fallen over and its vast trunk lay across the path. There was a faint track veering right which seemed to go round the end of the tree.

'Wow, cool,' said Archie, staring up at the huge circle of roots and soil and stones which had been pulled up when the tree fell. Lily bent down and picked up a stone.

'Mum's going to love this,' she said, showing it to me. It was a large phallic-shaped piece of flint. I grinned.

'Let's see,' said Archie.

'It's just a stone,' I told him.

He grabbed it. 'It looks like a big willy if you ask me,' he said.

Lily and I fell about laughing. Lily took the flint back and we carried on.

Just as Archie was beginning to complain, the trees stopped abruptly. There was no fence or wall and we found ourselves staring out across a huge field.

The field was bordered by hedges, beyond which were more fields. The field on the right had cows in it and I was relieved to see that the gate between our field and theirs was closed. I didn't like cows very much. I didn't like the way they stood and stared and I'd heard about people out walking their dogs who had been trampled to death by them. The field on the left was bare and had been ploughed into stripes of brown soil.

'What's that?' said Archie.

We looked to where he was pointing. On the other side of our field the ground rose slightly into a bank. It looked circular and at the top of the bank on one side was a brick structure. We crossed the field towards it.

As we got closer we could see that the whole thing was bigger than it looked from the other side of the field. The grass bank rose steeply and we couldn't see what was over the top. The brick thing was square with a concrete slab on the top of it. We could see graffiti all round the edges.

'Let's have our picnic up there,' said Lily and started scrambling up the bank. When she reached the top she stopped suddenly. 'Whoa, come and look at this.'

Archie got there first. 'Eew, yuk!' I heard him say. I crawled up the last bit and looked over the top.

Chapter Fourteen

On Saturday morning I told Mum I was going into town to meet up with some friends. Lily sat on her bed and watched me getting ready but we didn't talk. I didn't want to tell her anything about my new friends and I guessed, from her silence, that she didn't want to know.

We were only going to Posh Nosh and then round the shops so I put on a pair of jeans and my favourite top. I was about to shut the wardrobe door when I caught sight of myself in the long mirror on the inside of the door. The truth is, ever since The Incident, I've tried not to look in the mirror if I can help it. It's as if I don't want to come face to face with myself any more. As it was, I wasn't looking myself in the eye. I was just looking to see if my jeans and top combo would do. I decided it wouldn't; it needed something else.

One of Lily's Indian scarves had fallen to the bottom of the wardrobe. I picked it up and put it on. I didn't look in the mirror again so I didn't know if I looked good in it or not. But I thought Lily always looked nice in it, and if she did then I should too. I turned round fully expecting Lily to tell me to take her scarf off but she didn't. She just stared at me so I said 'Cheerio', and walked out of the room. I was about to go into the sitting room to find Mum and tell her I was going, when there was a knock on the door.

'Are you ready?'

It was Effy. I hadn't arranged that she would come round and pick me up. I was about to tell her that I'd spoken to Devlin and he couldn't come when Mum walked in.

'Are you off then, girls?' she said.

'Yes, we've just got to pick up Devlin first,' explained Effy.

Damn. Now it was too late. Mum would know I hadn't talked to Devlin about going out.

'Have fun,' said Mum. She came over to me and started fussing with the scarf round my neck. I tensed up but then she kissed me and said, 'Take care.'

When we got to the top of the basement steps I said to Effy, 'Look, I haven't actually asked Devlin if he can come or not.'

'Oh, okay, let's go and ask him then,' said Effy as if it was the simplest thing in the world and before I could stop her or warn her that he was probably going to be pretty hostile, she'd knocked on the front door.

Devlin's dad opened the door. I'd never met him before. He looked like Devlin, or more accurately Devlin looked like him. He had the same brown, wavy hair and blue eyes.

Effy was asking if Devlin was in. Devlin's dad, for some reason, was hugely amused that there were girls calling for him. He called for Devlin to come downstairs and when Devlin appeared his dad said, 'We've only been here a few weeks and already the girls are lining up at the door!'

Devlin went bright red.

'Yes, and there are three more dying to meet you,' said Effy.

'So what are you waiting for?' said Mr Wade.

I could plainly see Devlin's dilemma because it was similar to mine a minute ago. He couldn't make up an excuse because his dad was standing there and he'd know it wasn't true. I didn't dare look at Devlin. He'd hate me for this.

Devlin grabbed his jacket and we piled out the door. I was relieved when Effy took over and introduced herself. By the time we got to the café she'd found out that Devlin hadn't wanted to come to England (no offence), he'd tried to get his parents to let him stay with a friend but his mum wasn't having any of it and said it would do him good. But there weren't any baseball teams here and he was missing his friends. He didn't say anything about a girlfriend and I was willing Effy to ask but she didn't.

Effy was being very sympathetic. She was saying how

hard it must be for him and that she was sure it would get better once he'd settled in. She said she'd be terrified if she had to move to LA and leave all her friends behind. I thought that was pretty ironic really as she had more or less done just that. Okay, so our new school wasn't three thousand miles away, but it was a world away from St Bart's.

Molly, Katy and Harriet were waiting for us at the café. Posh Nosh was another irony. There was nothing posh about the café or what it served. It was a sort of health food place run by ageing hippies and it was always really busy because the food was good and not too expensive. All sorts of people came in here, from business men to the homeless, from school kids to pensioners.

We found a big table and ordered our drinks. I took a sneaky look at Devlin to see how he was coping in the company of five girls. He looked fine. In fact, he looked perfectly happy. None of the others were shy and they were all talking to him. By the time the drinks arrived they'd asked him what his best friend was called (Jake) and what his favourite subjects were at school (math and science) – they laughed at him for calling it math instead of maths. He told them about his dog (Gimbo) who'd died last year and how hard it was because they'd been together since Devlin was two and how much he missed him. They even found out which was his favourite baseball team (Angels of Anaheim), as if they knew anything about baseball. Which they obviously didn't because they said the Angels of Anaheim sounded like a really good fantasy film. Devlin took it well.

I sat and listened and got more and more depressed as I realised that Devlin was actually really chatty and friendly and fun to be with – obviously it *was* only me that he had a problem with.

The girls wanted to know if Americans were really like the ones in the films or on *Friends* or all the other sitcoms they'd seen. Devlin just laughed and asked whether British people were like the ones on the television here and they had to admit they weren't really – not even on the 'reality' programmes because even those people weren't 'normal', they were all acting up for the cameras.

It was impossible to stay depressed for long, though, and everyone was calling me Emily which was nice because today I really felt like Emily for the first time.

I went to the toilet and when I was washing my hands Harriet came in.

'Why didn't you tell us how gorgeous he is?' she said, checking her face in the mirror. 'I'd have made more of an effort if I'd known.' Our eyes met in the mirror. 'Oh, I see,' she said.

'What?'

'Don't worry, I'll tell the others to back off.' And before I could put her straight, she'd gone. When I got back to the table Devlin looked up and smiled at me and it wasn't until he looked away and started talking to Harriet that I realised I'd forgotton to smile back. Now he'd think it was me who was being unfriendly.

After we'd eaten we hit the shops. I was expecting Devlin to make some excuse and go off home but he seemed perfectly happy to hang out with us.

We bought a frisbee and ended up on the green at the Royal Crescent. While it wasn't exactly hot, with it being autumn, the sun was out and there wasn't any wind. There were loads of people dotted over the grass, kicking footballs about or just sitting around. It was the sort of thing that Lily would have enjoyed and I felt guilty.

Then it was time to go to Katy's for the marathon film night.

'You can come too,' Katy told Devlin. He politely declined and said it sounded great but he'd better get back or his parents would think he'd been kidnapped. I thought that was very tactful as he was probably thinking there was no way he was going to spend the evening watching a load of girlie films.

When Effy's dad dropped me home it was pretty late, but Mum was waiting up for me.

We had a drink in the kitchen while I told her all about my day. When I finally went to bed it was very quiet in our room. I looked over at Lily's bed. I unwound her scarf from my neck and laid it on the end of her bed. 'Thanks,' I whispered into the darkness, but there was no reply.

As I got undressed I realised that I felt happy. It was the first time since The Incident that I'd truly felt happy. I was filled with a sense of panic. Shakily, I climbed into bed and got my journal out. If I finished writing about The Incident I'd quash any happy feelings. It felt wrong to be happy.

I climbed up the last bit of the slope and reached the other two at the top. We were standing on the brim of a gigantic bowl. A bowl full of mud soup.

'What is it?' said Archie.

'I think it's some sort of reservoir,' I said, though it wasn't like anything I'd ever seen before. Somebody had dug out a huge dip in the ground and lined it with bricks. I reckoned that most of the earth that had been dug out had been used to make the bank that ran round the edge. The square brick structure with the concrete top must house some sort of pump, I thought. I guessed it was pretty old, Victorian or something by the look of the bricks. They were small and worn with age.

'Anyhow,' I told Archie, 'it's not in use any more.' That was stating the obvious. Rather than being filled with water, as I supposed it was meant to be, it was half full of gunk. It looked like black, peaty mud topped with a thick layer of leaves and branches that had soaked up so much moisture that they were all black and had turned to a pulpy mess. There was a strong smell coming off it but it wasn't unpleasant. It was earthy and woody. The peat soup came halfway up the brick incline, though judging by the slimy marks at intervals down the side, it was slowly drying up.

'Whatever,' said Lily, looking totally unimpressed. 'I want my lunch.'

The obvious place to have it was on top of the graffiti-covered brick cube. We helped Archie up, then climbed up ourselves. We sat with our backs to the brick bowl, looking out towards the woods instead. I scanned the tree line but couldn't see any sign of the boys. Blue Hoodie must have gone into the pub with his mates after all.

Chapter Fifteen

I was sitting at the kitchen table doing my homework when I heard the squeak of the gate at the top of the basement steps. I looked up and saw Devlin coming down the stairs. I jumped up and opened the door before he could knock.

'Hi,' I said. No marks for originality.

I hadn't seen Devlin for a couple of weeks, not since we'd been out to Posh Nosh. I'd wondered what he'd been doing and I'd even crept up the stairs a couple of times and pressed my ear to the door to see if I could hear anything, but guilt and a fear of being seen by Lily put a stop to that.

Of course the girls kept asking me about him and they'd spent a couple of lunchtimes trying to come up with a plot to see him again without being too obvious. But short of going round and knocking on his door and asking for him, nobody had had any bright ideas.

I moved aside so he could come in, but then I spotted a leaflet he was clutching in his hand and I realised he'd probably just come down to put it through the door and hadn't planned on talking to me. The look of embarrassment on his face confirmed my suspicion and wiped the welcoming smile off my face.

He held the leaflet out. It was advertising some upcoming lectures at the university.

'Dad thought your mom might be interested in going,' Devlin said.

I took the leaflet from him. 'She's not in at the moment.'

There was an awkward silence. Devlin ran his fingers through his hair.

'Look, can I come in?'

I opened the door wider and he came inside. As he walked past I could smell his shampoo, or deodorant or something. Whatever it was, it was nice.

The awkward silence was there again and I wondered what he wanted.

'Do you want a drink?' I said to fill the gap.

'Yeah, thanks. Have you got any Coke?'

'No, sorry.' I didn't want to go into an explanation about Mum's dislike of that particular drink and how she was always saying she'd rather we drank beer than Coke. It would probably make him think she was deranged or something. I tried to remember my manners. 'We've got tea, coffee or . . .' I opened the fridge and peered inside. ' . . . guava juice.'

'I'll try the coffee,' he said, so I switched the kettle on. Devlin sat down at the table.

'Homework?' he said, looking at my school books. Full marks for deduction.

'Yes, I have to write about the worst day of my life.'

God, what was I prattling on for? I could have just said yes.

'So what are you writing about then? The day you had to show me around town?'

He was grinning at me. I smiled back. 'Yeah, how did you guess?'

'I'm really sorry about that. I've wanted to apologise for ages but I've been too embarrassed.'

I didn't know what to say so I just looked at him. He'd picked up my pen and was fiddling with it, popping the end in and out.

'The truth is . . .' Devlin started to say then stopped.

The truth was what? That he didn't like me? That the very thought of me repelled him?

'What?'

'The truth is . . . I . . . The thing is . . .'

Whatever the problem was he was having real trouble getting it out. You know when someone has a stammer and they can't get the word out and the urge to finish the sentence for them is overwhelming?

'You don't like me. It's okay, it's fine, don't worry about it,' I blurted out.

Devlin looked puzzled.

'No, you've got it wrong, it's not that . . . I do like you! It's just that . . . Right, the thing is . . .'

'For God's sake – just spit it out will you!' I was flustered because he'd said he liked me.

'I'm trying to! You keep interrupting me!'

'Sorry,' I said, 'I won't say another word.'

'Right. I've got a kind of problem and it sounds pretty stupid but I can't help it . . .'

Oh no, he was going to tell me all about his girlfriend back home. I didn't want to hear it.

'It's okay, it's fine . . .' I told him.

'You said you wouldn't interrupt!' Devlin was seriously exasperated now.

'Sorry,' I mumbled and mimed zipping up my mouth.

'Right . . . The truth is . . . and the reason I was acting so strange . . . Promise you won't laugh?'

Oh, for heaven's sake! I nodded at him.

'Okay, well . . . I'm aquaphobic.'

The last bit came out in a rush and because it wasn't what I'd been expecting him to say it took me a moment to understand.

'I don't get it,' I said. 'You were fine when we went out the other day – and we went to the park and everything.'

Now Devlin was looking confused. Then his face cleared. 'No, I said aquaphobic – not agoraphobic. I have a fear of water, not open spaces.'

'I don't get it.'

'I know, it's stupid, isn't it? I hate myself for it, believe me, but I can't help it.'

'Yeah, but I still don't get it.'

'You mean why I was so uptight when you showed me round town?'

'Yeah.'

'Well, first off you said we were going across a bridge. That can be a problem sometimes. As it turned out it was the best bridge I've ever seen because you can't see any water when you're crossing it so that turned out okay. Then you took me to the Roman Baths and when I saw what it was like on the leaflet I couldn't do it. I didn't want to be enclosed in a small space with all that water.' He looked embarrassed again.

'And then you suggested a river cruise,' he continued. 'By that time I was wondering if it was a wind up and Mom had told you about my problem and you were just having a laugh.'

'I'd never do that!' I interrupted.

'Yeah, well I know that now – now I know you better, but at the time I wasn't sure. And then . . .' he said, 'you asked me if I wanted to go swimming and that just about did it! I couldn't think of another way to say no. I knew I was coming over as rude but I couldn't help it.'

I thought back to that day and suddenly I started laughing.

'Hey, you promised not to laugh.' Devlin looked offended but I couldn't stop.

'Oh God, and then the café . . .' I spluttered, remembering his face when we came out beside the river.

'I'm sorry; I'm not laughing at you. I'm laughing because I never knew there were so many water-based activities – and I had to pick them all.'

Now Devlin was laughing too.

'Anyway, that's why I was behaving so weirdly. It wasn't because I didn't like you. Although, to be fair, I did go off you when you kept going back to the river.'

'Oh God, I didn't know! I'm really sorry. You should have told me!'

'Yeah, well, I'd only just met you and it's hard admitting it. I mean, I feel so stupid but I can't help it. It's pretty bad and there's absolutely no reason for it.'

'I see,' I said. 'I thought you didn't want to do anything because you didn't like me,' I finished up lamely.

Devlin said, 'Yeah, I realised that after I got home. I thought you must think I was really rude and ungrateful, you know – because you didn't know about my problem and why I kept saying I didn't want to do any of those things.'

'It must be awful,' I said. I didn't like spiders much, they made my skin crawl but it wasn't a full-blown phobia. I couldn't imagine what that would be like.

'I get by okay most of the time. Of course, I have to see a shrink. That's the best thing about coming here. I get a break from that. The last one I had was terrible; she tried to get me to face my fears. If anything it made it worse. It just fuelled my nightmares. I can avoid water all I want in the day but I have nightmares and I don't sleep much.'

I remembered that nightmare I'd had about the water

and Lily looking at me and not being able to breathe. I jumped up and took his mug.

I wanted to tell him about The Incident and how I understood about not sleeping and nightmares. I think I might have told him but he got in first.

'I came to apologise and I thought I might be able to make it up to you. I thought we could go out again, to a movie or something, and I promise not to behave like a jerk.'

'Okay,' I said, 'that would be great. I'd like that. Let's do that.' Shut up, I thought. Don't overdo it.

He was grinning at me again. 'It'll be great as long as they're not showing *Titanic* or *Jaws*.'

'Or *The Little Mermaid*.'

'Enough!' said Devlin, laughing and shuddering at the same time. He got up to go.

'How about Saturday, then? I'll come down and get you after lunch.'

'That's fine,' I said.

He opened the kitchen door. 'See ya,' he said, and was gone, taking the steps two at a time. I had that happy feeling again. Had he just asked me out? Was it a date or was he just being polite? I decided that this was probably just his way of saying sorry so there was no point in getting carried away. But he had said he liked me, hadn't he?

I pulled my homework towards me. Must concentrate. This was due in tomorrow. Mrs Clark had said something about reading them out in class. I didn't have a clue what to write. I knew it wasn't all that important; it wasn't going towards our grade or anything, but I'd have to come up with something in case she picked me. I'd written *The Worst Day* at the top of the page and it was taunting me.

I thought about my journal and how I'd nearly finished it. I was going to see Ted tomorrow after school. Suddenly I wanted to get it done; I wanted it out of the way. I wanted to be able to tell him I'd faced up to it. Damn Mrs Clark and her stupid homework. I'd just have to tell her I hadn't done it. What was the worst that could happen? A detention? Well, big deal.

I stuffed my school books back into my bag and got out my journal. I wrote *The Worst Day* at the top of the page and began to write.

It wasn't much of a lunch. Archie sat dipping his banana into his yoghurt while Lily and I peeled our boiled eggs. We tore off pieces of bread and squirted salad cream onto them. Lily missed and the salad cream ran down her wellie boot, which Archie thought was hilarious for some reason, so Lily squirted some onto his chocolate biscuit, which he didn't find so funny. But he did let us share his packet of biscuits. Then we realised we'd forgotten to bring a drink and we were all claggy from the chocolate biscuits. Lily ate the apple and I shared the satsuma with Archie, which helped a bit. Then we rolled down the bank. Archie wanted to do it again and again. Lily and I left him to it and we lay on our backs in the grass watching the clouds and trying to find pictures in them.

'There's a face,' said Lily, pointing at a shifting, thin cloud. 'Oh, it's gone, did you see it?'

'That's a dragon, look! There.'

Archie had stopped rolling and was looking for stones in the long grass which he could throw into the muddy bowl.

'No, it's not a dragon, it's a train,' said Lily.

I was trying to see what she meant when I heard a crashing from the woods. I sat up so I could hear it better. I remembered the sign on the gate saying No Admittance. Was it the boys or was it an irate farmer?

Lily heard it too and obviously decided it was Blue Hoodie and his mates.

'Let's go back now,' she said. I knew what she was thinking. She wanted to flaunt herself at the boys again. As if they'd be interested. She seemed to have forgotten that she was wearing wellies and an old duffle coat.

'Let's wait a bit,' I said, unsure what to do. It hadn't been much of an adventure and I was getting worried in case no one at home had found the note we'd left. Mum wasn't the neurotic type and wouldn't have worried about me and Lily going off for the day, but I wasn't so sure about Archie's parents. We might be in real trouble when we got back. On the other hand, I didn't really fancy entering the woods if the boys were in there. I don't know why; they just made me nervous.

'Well, I'm going,' said Lily, standing up. She picked up the rucksack and put the stone that we'd got for Mum into it and then handed the bag back to me.

'I'm not carrying that,' I told her. 'The stone was your idea so you can carry it.'

Lily tried to put the bag on but it wouldn't fit over her duffle coat.

'You'll have to lengthen the straps,' I said. She pulled them until they were at their longest and tried again. She got it on but it was a tight fit.

I turned round to call Archie, but I couldn't see him anywhere.

Chapter Sixteen

I didn't finish writing in my journal until three o'clock in the morning. Then I slept until my alarm went off at seven forty-five. Tired doesn't begin to describe how I felt. I wondered about telling Mum I wasn't feeling well and taking the day off. But in the end I dragged myself out of bed and got ready for school. I put the journal in my bag because, although I knew Ted didn't want to read it, I wanted to show it to him anyhow.

Writing the final bit last night was the hardest thing I'd ever had to do, but now I'd done it and it felt like I'd done something important. I worried briefly about the fact that I hadn't done my homework, but that seemed so unimportant in the light of what I *had* managed to do that I brushed it aside and went to get the bus.

At lunchtime I nearly told the others about the visit I'd

had from Devlin and the fact that he'd asked me to go to the cinema with him. I didn't, though, because I knew they'd get all excited, thinking I had a date with him and I didn't want to have to explain. It would mean telling them about the disastrous day we'd had and about his phobia and everything, so in the end I decided to keep quiet.

The last lesson of the day was RS with Mrs Clark. Effy and I got there a bit late because our previous lesson had run over. Mrs Clark was already there and she told us to hurry up and sit down. My hopes of sitting at the back and dozing off were ruined because the only two seats left were on the front table and one of the seats was next to Amy. I sidled in first so that Effy didn't have to sit next to her.

The lesson was about worldwide disasters, political and celebrity scandals and how they were portrayed in the media. I think we were meant to be thinking about 'truth' and the angles the media chose when narrating the stories and whether or not they could be trusted. Then we were meant to think about how the internet had changed reporting and how the public were now all involved with mobile phone cameras and social network sites.

To tell the truth, I wasn't listening that closely because I was so tired. Then it occurred to me that the longer Mrs Clark talked, the less time there'd be to discuss our homework. There'd never be time for everyone to read their stuff out, so I asked a couple of questions to try and prolong the discussion. I'd tell Mrs Clark at the end of the lesson that I hadn't done the homework; I just didn't want to have to explain in front of the whole class.

When she finally asked who was going to start by reading out their own 'worst day' there was very little enthusiasm. So she picked on a girl who'd written about how her mum had gone into hospital and her dad had forgotten her tenth birthday because he was too busy and worried about her mum. She said she kept waiting for him to say something or give her a present, but he never did and she didn't like to ask. Then she started thinking that maybe there was going to be a surprise party or something so she got all dressed up, but it never happened and she went to bed and cried herself to sleep.

The spin, or up-side of the story, was that her mum got better and then she got double presents when her mum found out she hadn't had a birthday.

Then it was the turn of the girl who'd got fake goods for Christmas.

After that was a girl who started going on about her boyfriend and how she'd found out he was seeing someone else when she'd walked in on them at a party. There was a bit of sniggering during this one, but the girl wasn't taking it very seriously and I began to wonder if it was even true. I suppose that was the point. We were meant to be questioning what we were told by the media after all. The girl ended up throwing her drink all over the couple.

I was watching the clock and trying to keep a low profile so the teacher didn't pick on me. But then her gaze fell on our table. I held my breath.

'Amy, let's hear your contribution.'

I let my breath out, but I didn't relax because Amy never did her homework so she was unlikely to have anything. I slid down in my seat so Mrs Clark wouldn't move on to me next. But Amy was standing up and looking pleased with herself. I hoped whatever she had was long because it was ten minutes until the end of the lesson. Amy started to read.

'*The Worst Day*,' she said in a dramatic voice. Then:

'*I called Archie's name, looking round wildly for him.*

'*"Milly, help!" The voice was coming from beyond the bank, from inside the bowl. Lily and I scrambled up the slope and peered over the edge.*

'*It was instantly clear what had happened. Archie's yoghurt pot had rolled down the inside of the bowl and come to rest on the black sludge where its whiteness stood out starkly against the black. He'd obviously thought he could retrieve it and had gone down after it, but there was no footing on the slimy bricks and he was pressed against the side with his feet resting in the mud.*'

It took a minute for me to realise what Amy was reading. I couldn't believe it. I could hear the words coming out of her mouth and I knew they were mine but I was gripped by a horrible fascination to hear them coming from somebody else, like it didn't have anything to do with me any more.

'*"Oh, Archie, for heaven's sake," said Lily. She sat on the rim and leaned over the edge and tried to reach him.*'

A small part of my brain was thinking dispassionately that Amy had a very good reading voice for someone who pretended to be so stupid.

"'Listen, Archie. I want you to raise one of your arms above your head." Archie was as stiff as a board with his arms firmly clamped by his sides.

'I joined Lily and lay on my front, carefully keeping most of my weight behind me. I didn't intend to end up with my head in the muck.

'I couldn't help myself from twisting round and taking one more look towards the wood. I definitely saw a flash of blue against the green. The boys had followed us after all. I was about to tell Lily. Perhaps we could call to them and they could help us get Archie out. But then I thought, they've been in the pub and probably had a couple of pints. I remembered how they'd pointed and leered at us.'

Amy sniggered. I immediately snapped out of my daze.

What was Amy doing with my journal? She must have taken it from my bag which was on the floor between our chairs. She was holding up the turquoise notebook with the butterflies and flowers on the cover. She was reading out my private journal.

'Hey, that's mine!' I said, making a grab for it.

'Girls!' said Mrs Clark.

'She's got my . . . that's my work.'

'Is this Emily's?' said Mrs Clark. Amy was grinning like she'd done something really clever. 'Give it back,' sighed the teacher.

Amy made a face, threw the notebook onto the table in front of me and sat back down.

'Right, perhaps you could have your turn now,' Mrs Clark said to me.

'I'm sorry,' I told her, 'I haven't done it.'

'Come along,' said Mrs Clark as if I hadn't said anything. 'Stop holding everyone up.'

'It was rubbish anyway,' said Amy. 'What was it anyhow? *The Day I Lost My Yoghurt*? No, don't tell me – it was *The Day I Lost My Virginity*. To some drunk, randy boys.' The rest of the class were sniggering now, except Effy who looked worried.

I could feel the tears welling up but there was no way I was going to start crying. How dare *she* make fun of it. If only she knew! Glaring at Amy, I grabbed the journal from the table and started reading.

We could do this without any help from the boys.

'Archie,' I said. 'Just put one of your hands up so we can pull you out.'

Archie tried to look up at us and twisted slightly. He immediately slid a bit further into the sludge.

'Archie! Don't move!' Lily yelled.

'You told me to,' wailed Archie.

'Milly said to put your arm up. Just do it!' Lily shouted.

Archie didn't move. She was scaring him. If he put his right arm up I could grab him. If it was his left, Lily would get him. I decided I probably had a better hold than Lily because I was lying down.

'Archie,' I said as calmly as I could, 'lift your right arm.'

Archie didn't move.

'I don't know which one that is,' he said.

I tried to remember back to when I was seven. 'Your right hand is the one you write with,' I told him.

Archie raised his left arm. I'd forgotten – he was left-handed. His arms seemed impossibly short. Lily lunged forward and managed to grab a handful of his sleeve and she pulled hard. The feeling must have given Archie courage because he raised his other arm and I got hold of his hand and yanked him up. I got a hold of his chest and shuffled backwards until we were both lying on the top of the bank. I sat up. Archie's feet were soaking wet and covered in a thick layer of black mud. He'd begun to cry.

I turned to Lily. 'Have you seen the state of his feet? How are we going to . . .' I stopped. Lily wasn't there.

'Milly, I slipped.'

Oh, great. Now we'd have to do it all over again, I thought as I peered over the side just in time to see Lily gently sliding down the bricks. At least she's got wellies on I thought as her feet hit the sludge. I expected her to come to a stop like Archie had, but she didn't. She just carried on; she was a lot heavier than Archie and she'd been leaning forward slightly. Her wellies disappeared beneath the surface.

'Oh, yuk,' she said, 'this isn't mud, it's water!'

I could see now that the layer of leaves and mud and twigs wasn't solid like I'd thought, it was just a covering on top of the water.

I sat on the edge and leaned over but I couldn't reach Lily.

'I'm coming down,' I told her.

'No, don't! Don't go in there.' Archie was sobbing.

'He's right, don't,' said Lily. 'He won't be able to get us both out.'

Lily was up to her knees and still sinking. Her wellies must have filled with water by now and the added weight was pulling her in faster. She just kept going. I remember how slowly everything seemed to be happening but it was so quick at the same time. One minute she was sliding and the next she was in up to her waist.

I turned round and started yelling at the wood. 'Help!' I yelled it three times. Nothing. No flash of blue, no sound at all. I turned back to Lily.

She was trying to turn round so she was facing the bricks. I suppose she thought she could get a better hold that way, but there was no hold on the slope and by the time she was facing me she was in up to her armpits. She was trying to keep her arms out of the water but trying to reach forwards towards the slope at the same time. I could see the water soaking into the heavy wool of the duffle coat, and all the time she was slipping further in.

'Lily, take the rucksack off.' My voice came out as a sob. This couldn't be happening.

Lily tried shrugging the bag off but it was too tight. As she reached back to pull it off she disappeared under the water.

'Archie, quick! Listen to me! I want you to run to the

woods, as fast as you can, and get a big stick. Like a branch. And Archie,' I added in desperation, 'if you can find those boys we saw on the bus, bring them back with you.'

Archie stared at me, his eyes wide and terrified.

'Go!' I yelled at him and he ran, slipping down the bank and stumbling over the long grass of the field.

Lily came up gasping. She had leaves and twigs stuck in her hair.

'I . . . There's mud on the bottom . . . except it's not the bottom. Milly, I can't . . .' She went under again.

I started to move down the inside of the bowl. My trainers had a grip on the top part where the bricks were driest but they wouldn't hold on the slimy part. Lily came back up.

'Milly, don't! Please.'

I hesitated. We stared at each other. I was crying but Lily looked strangely calm. There might have been tears on her face but I couldn't be sure. A strand of wet hair was stuck to her face. Our eyes were locked for what seemed like a lifetime. It was a lifetime; our lifetime, together. Then she was gone.

I waited for her to come back up. The sun came out from behind a cloud and a flock of rooks rose up. Their cawing filled my head. It sounded urgent and harsh.

I waited.

Nothing happened.

'Lily!' Could she hear me, under there? 'Lily, please.' In my head I was running into the woods, looking for Archie, telling him to hurry up, grabbing the branch off him, running back.

But I couldn't move. I couldn't take my eyes off the pond. Every second that passed I thought would be the one where Lily reappeared. I'd kill her. She was playing a trick on me. It wasn't funny.

On the surface of the pond the leaves and twigs that had been disturbed by Lily thrashing about were shifting back together, like nothing had ever happened.

'Lily,' I whispered. The sun disappeared behind a cloud.

I waited. She had to come back up. People didn't drown like that. They got swept into the sea by giant waves or washed away by floods. They didn't just sink into stagnant ponds. Not when they were twins; one half of a whole. Not when their twin was sitting on the bank, waiting for them to come back up.

If she wouldn't come up then I'd have to go down. She was probably waiting for me.

'Lily, I'm coming,' I said.

I swallowed and looked up briefly. Everyone was sitting very still and all eyes were fixed on me. But I couldn't stop now.

'Milly! I'm coming!'

Archie was racing across the field. He came panting up the bank.

'I did what you said. I found the boys.' I looked beyond him and saw the three boys from the bus coming out of the woods.

'Come on. Quick!' shouted Archie. The boys weren't running but they walked a bit faster. The one in the blue hoodie

was about five paces in front of the other two.

'Where's Lily?' said Archie, looking around, like she might be hiding behind the brick box where we'd had lunch.

I was still staring at the surface of the pond. The boys came up the bank.

'What's the problem then?' said one of them.

'Lily fell in the pond,' said Archie.

'So where is she?' That was the other one. He didn't look too bright.

'Is this some sort of joke?' said the first one.

The boy in the blue hoodie was watching me. I think the fact that I was sitting there, like I was daydreaming or something was making them think there was nothing wrong. Blue Hoodie bent down so I could see his face out of the corner of my eye.

'Where's your sister?' he said.

I pointed.

'How long?'

I shrugged. He was undoing his belt. He started asking the others if they were wearing belts. Only one of them was. He put the end of one belt through the buckle of the other and pulled on them. The other two boys had caught on and I could hear them trying to decide what would be the best thing to do.

'Josh, you're the lightest, we'll lower you down,' said one of the boys to Blue Hoodie. Josh was taking his hoodie off. He turned to the dopey-looking boy. 'Ring the police.'

He wrapped the end of the belt round his wrist. The bigger of the other two boys lay on his front holding the other end. The other one got his mobile out and started tapping in the number.

149

When Josh got to the bottom he started feeling around in the water. At first he resisted getting his feet wet, then he was in up to his knees. He felt further out. His arm was wet up to the shoulder. He slid further in until there was no more belt left and the water was up to the top of his legs.

'Can you feel anything?' said his mate.

Josh didn't reply, he just kept on trying; reaching out under the water with his spare arm. His friend shuffled forwards, leaning over the side until only his legs were on the bank.

'Here, Charlie, sit on my legs,' he shouted at the third boy. Charlie was trying to explain to the person on the other end of the phone where we were but he sat down, pinning the big lad's legs to the ground. Josh was up to his waist now and still trying to find Lily under the surface. He kept trying for half an hour before the police turned up and pulled him out. They prised the belt away from his swollen hand.

I couldn't move. It was like my whole body had just stopped working. I could feel my heart beating in my chest, I could hear it pulsing in my ears. Josh came over and put his blue hoodie round my shoulders. Then I heard him talking to a policeman.

'We saw them come in here. I was worried, it's no place for kids, so instead of getting the bus we came in here to check on them. The little boy found us; told us what had happened . . . If only we hadn't gone to the pub . . .'

I was led away by a policewoman. I wanted to stay. I wanted to be there for Lily, she'd need me. But my jaw wouldn't work. My mouth was clamped shut and I couldn't think of the right words to say anyway.

We crossed the field. Archie was holding my hand and I could hear a helicopter. We went through the woods, round the fallen-down tree and through the rusty gate that was now standing open. There was a fire engine in the road and I wondered why. They put me in an ambulance.

I didn't see the boys again until the inquest. I never saw Lily again. I wanted to go with Mum when she went to identify her, but Mum said I mustn't. She said it was best if I remembered Lily how she was: before.

Chapter Seventeen

The bell rang. I glanced up briefly and was met by a wall of shocked faces.

I looked at Mrs Clark. She was staring at the top of her desk as if it was the most interesting thing in the world. Her cheeks looked damp. Well, that would teach her to set stupid homework.

Amy was examining her fingernails and was the only person in the room, apart from Mrs Clark, who wasn't staring at me. I looked at Effy. She looked right back and I saw it. Pity. Right there in her eyes.

I ran.

I ran down the corridor and into the nearest loo and locked myself in the cubicle. I was still clutching my journal.

I started crying. I was crying because I'd just ruined

Emily. I'd shown everyone Milly and now when they looked at me they wouldn't see Emily any more, they'd see half a twin.

Once I'd started crying I couldn't stop and then I was crying because I missed Lily. I missed Lily so much it hurt. When people talk about heartache they're not wrong. My heart was aching, literally. I curled myself up around it.

Girls came into the toilets and stood around the mirrors putting make-up on. I stuffed my fist into my mouth and waited for them to go. When it was quiet I took my hand away and let the rasping sobs come. I hated Mrs Clark for being such a fool. No experienced teacher would have set that homework. I hated Amy for being such a cow and goading me into reading the journal. I hated Lily for not trying harder to get out and for leaving me. But most of all I hated myself.

I hated myself for not telling Archie he couldn't come with us on that day and for not telling Lily she couldn't go into the woods and for making her carry the bag with the stone in it.

I blew my nose on some toilet roll. I didn't need to look in the mirror to know that my nose and eyes must be red and swollen. I didn't want to leave the cubicle but the cleaning staff would be in soon and I didn't want them to find me here.

I closed my eyes. I was so tired.

I was tired of never being able to sleep because when I

shut my eyes all I saw was Lily standing at the end of my bed in a waterlogged duffle coat with leaves and twigs in her hair, looking at me.

I was tired of pretending to Mum that I was okay and that I wasn't crippled with guilt every time I smiled or felt happy.

I was tired of Mum pretending to me that she wasn't wishing every day it was me and not Lily who had drowned.

I was tired of pretending to be Emily.

But most of all I was tired of pretending that Lily was still here; about to come down the basement steps. I was tired of pretending she was in the chair or sitting in her bed, talking to me and watching me.

I was tired of not facing up to the fact that she was gone.

And I didn't know what to do about any of it and I'd never felt so lonely in my life.

I opened the cubicle door. Effy was leaning on the sink.

I scoured her expression for signs of pity but I couldn't detect anything.

I thought, *If she says something cheerful I'm going to hit her.*

'I've got your bag,' said Effy. Then she crossed the floor and gave me a hug. I thought I might start crying again but it seemed I'd cried myself out. Effy let go.

'I've rung my dad. He's coming to pick us up and take you home.'

I nodded. Good old practical Effy.

'I knew, you know,' said Effy, when we were sitting on the wall waiting for her dad.

'What do you mean?'

Effy looked embarrassed. 'When we first met and I mentioned you to my mum she said the name sounded familiar. I Googled it and it came up with the news story. You know, it was in all the papers.'

I had known but I hadn't looked at any of them.

'You never said.' I thought back to Effy chatting away about her problems and wondered if she'd just been filling a huge gap caused by my silence.

'I thought you'd tell me when you were ready,' said Effy.

'I wasn't ready,' I said, 'and now everyone knows.'

'Bloody Amy,' said Effy.

I nodded.

In the car I remembered I was supposed to be going to Ted's. I'd get Mum to ring him when I got home and tell him I wasn't coming today. I really wanted to see Mum. I should be talking to Mum, not Ted.

Effy's dad stopped the car outside our house. Effy squeezed my hand. 'Ring me if you want, later.'

I nodded and squeezed her hand back to show that I was grateful to her.

I went down the basement steps but stopped with my hand on the door handle. Before I went in I made a promise to myself that I was going to accept the fact that

Lily had gone and stop pretending she was in there. Also, I was going to have a proper talk with Mum.

The kitchen was very tidy. It looked like Mum had given it a thorough clean. That could only mean one thing. She was putting off getting down to work. I switched the kettle on, deciding that I would have a cup of coffee and then I was going to go and sort out my room.

The last time I tried to do it Mum had come in.

'What are you doing?' she'd said, standing in the doorway.

I'd paused. I was holding one of Lily's skirts in my hand. It was an Indian, embroidered skirt with tiny bells hanging off the drawstrings. Very ethnic and very Lily. My hand shook slightly and the bells jingled in the silence, almost like Lily was contributing to the discussion.

'I'm just having a sort out.'

I'd been putting all Lily's things from the floor onto her bed. I planned to clear the floor and Hoover it, and then I was going to put some of Lily's stuff into boxes and put them under the bed. It wasn't easy. I'd been building up to it for ages.

'Don't,' said Mum. I'd looked at her. 'Lily wouldn't like it,' she'd said.

She was right. Lily wouldn't have liked it. *If she'd been here.*

So I'd thrown everything back onto the floor and it had been there ever since. Like she was still here. Like she could walk through the door any minute. Perhaps that's when I'd started to pretend that Lily *was* still here, I couldn't really remember.

But none of it was helping. It wasn't like I wanted to eradicate all signs of Lily, I just needed to clear the floor and tidy up a bit. Surely Mum could understand that. It wasn't like I was asking her to get rid of the stuff or asking her to get rid of Lily's bed. That's what I hated most: Lily's empty bed. But getting rid of it would be too much. I tried to imagine asking Effy over for the weekend and having her sleep in it. I knew I wasn't ready for that yet.

One step at a time. I think I'd just taken the first step.

I suddenly remembered Ted and the fact that I was meant to be there. I'd better ring him or better still get Mum to do it. I made her a cup of tea and it wasn't until I was pouring the milk that I began to wonder if she was even in. If she thought I was going to Ted's, perhaps she'd gone out. It was very quiet.

I found Mum in the sitting room, asleep on the sofa.

'Mum, I've brought you some tea.'

How was I going to explain that I wasn't at Ted's without telling her about the awful lesson and the journal and everything? I wasn't sure if I could face that right now, I felt washed out and a bit shaky.

Should I leave her to sleep and ring Ted myself? Mum might not wake up for a couple of hours and then she'd never know I hadn't made it to Ted's. I could do with a sleep myself. I went to put her tea on the side table and that was when I saw the empty pill bottle and the empty bottle of whisky.

I panicked. I'm not entirely sure what happened next. I think I instinctively ran upstairs to get help but I used the stairs indoors; the ones that were covered in things. I clambered over the stuff but when I got to the top the door was locked. I was banging on it and calling out for help. Then the door opened and a very shocked Devlin was standing there.

I must have been gabbling because he said, 'Slow down, start again,' but I was beyond speech so I gestured for him to follow me and stumbled back down the stairs.

I remember shaking Mum and her not waking up, at which point I must have got a bit rough with the shaking because Devlin pulled me off. He bent over her. 'It's okay,' he said, 'she's still breathing, but I think we should call the emergency services.'

I was on my knees by the sofa saying, 'Mum, Mum,' over and over again so Devlin found the phone and tried to ring for an ambulance.

'Do I call 911?' said Devlin.

'No, it's 999,' I managed to tell him. I was holding Mum's hand and rubbing it, willing her to wake up.

'Shouldn't we be doing something? Like making her throw up or walk around the room?' I said. I hated just sitting there.

'The ambulance will be here soon,' said Devlin. He looked really worried.

'I'm sorry,' I said. It was our fault he'd got dragged into this.

'Hey, it's not your fault,' he said, sitting down next to me and taking my hand. I couldn't look at him. Of course it was my fault. It was all my fault. Everything.

'Hello!' The voice was coming from the top of the stairs.

'Oh, thank God, my mom's back,' said Devlin, not even trying to hide his relief. 'I won't be long,' he said, getting up. 'I'll be right back.'

Chapter Eighteen

When Devlin's mum came in I had to move away so she could get a good look at Mum. Then the ambulance crew arrived and they surrounded Mum. I don't know what they were saying. It was like my brain had had enough for one day and had shut down. But Devlin never left my side until they loaded Mum into the ambulance. There was no way they were going to shut the doors on me. I scrambled in after the stretcher. There was a moment's confusion while the ambulance man tried to persuade me to get out and follow along in a taxi, and I remember refusing and the ambulance woman said it wouldn't do any harm.

But when we got to the hospital they hustled Mum away. A nurse told me to go and sit in a waiting room. Then another nurse came and asked me a load of questions about Mum.

'When can I see her?' I said.

'I don't know, but I'll keep you informed,' said the nurse.

It wasn't until she'd gone and I'd been by myself for what seemed like for ever, sitting in the uncomfortable plastic chair, that the realisation hit me. I was alone. Literally. David and Jeanie were thousands of miles away and apart from them, if something happened to Mum, I had no one. What would happen to me? Would I be sent to live with Eileen and Frank in Wimbledon? Mum had said they were very elderly so probably not.

I looked around, like I might find the answer somewhere, anywhere. I should have been at home now, talking to Mum about what had happened today, and instead I was sitting alone in a smelly hospital with Mum possibly dying down the corridor and no one to help me.

I stood up. I wanted to go home. How could Mum have done this to me? I could hardly breathe, I was so outraged at her selfishness. I knew she was hurting about Lily but so was I. Had I tried to kill myself? I admit I'd wished I was dead a few times since the accident because I didn't know how I was going to live without Lily, but I'd never considered killing myself because of what it would have done to Mum if I had.

I didn't think I could face Mum if she wasn't dead. I was so angry at her I might kill her myself. I left the waiting room and took off down the corridor, following the exit signs.

I suddenly realised I had nothing with me – no coat, no money, no phone and no key to the house. I couldn't even leave. My vision was blurred now by tears but I couldn't stop walking. I turned a corner, not caring if it was the right one or not.

'Hey!'

It was Devlin. Five minutes ago I'd have been overjoyed to see a familiar face but now I was in such a state I couldn't talk to anyone.

'Hey,' said Devlin again, only quieter this time. He held on to my upper arms to stop me from storming past. 'Milly, it's me, Devlin.' There were some chairs along the wall of the corridor and he led me towards them. All my resistance left me and I burst into tears.

'Oh no, what's happened? Your mom . . . Is she . . .?' He couldn't bring himself to finish the sentence.

'I . . . don't . . . know . . .' I managed.

'Listen, my mom will be along in a minute, she's looking for a doctor.' Devlin was talking slowly and gently to me, as though I was a small child, which was fine by me because that's what I felt like. 'We came straight away in a taxi. Dad's at home making up a bed for you. You can't sleep on your own in the flat if they keep your mom in overnight. Mom'll find out what's going on. If anyone can kick ass, it's my mother.' His attempt to cheer me up just made me cry all the harder. Devlin put his arm round me and I cried on his shoulder – literally. I soaked his shirt.

But he was right about his mum. She sure kicked some ass.

Devlin and I waited in the waiting room while she did it. I'd stopped crying but we didn't talk. I guess we were too busy worrying. But at least I wasn't on my own any more.

Mrs Wade came back. 'Your mum's fine. You can go and see her now.'

All thoughts of leaving without seeing her vanished. I couldn't get in there fast enough.

I was shown into a small side ward and saw Mum propped up in a bed. She was attached to a drip and looked more pale and fragile than I thought it was possible for anyone to look and still be alive.

I went and stood beside her bed but I couldn't think what to say, so I reached out and took her hand. Mum's eyelids flickered open.

'Milly?'

'I'm here, Mum.'

'Oh Milly, I'm so sorry.'

I let go of her hand. I couldn't think what to say.

'They're insisting on keeping me in overnight,' said Mum. 'It's pretty embarrassing really.'

'Embarrassing! You nearly die and you think it's embarrassing!' All the rage I'd felt earlier came flooding back. I'd just spent the evening on a roller coaster of emotions and embarrassment hadn't exactly been one of them.

Mum looked at me. 'I didn't nearly die! Who told you that?'

'I found you, Mum! You know, with the empty pill bottle and the empty whisky bottle!'

'Shhh!' Mum whispered, glancing round the ward. I

163

hadn't meant to yell but I couldn't help it. She took hold of my hand.

'Oh, Milly, I'm sorry . . . I didn't realise that's what you thought.' A tear rolled down her cheek and she brushed it away impatiently. 'The pill bottle was empty because I'd got to the end of it, not because I'd taken them all. That's why I overdid it on the whisky. I'm sorry . . . really sorry. I swear it won't happen again. I'm never touching another drop of whisky as long as I live, I promise.'

My hand was trembling and Mum pulled me towards her and gave me a hug. It was a bit awkward because of the drip but I hugged her back tight.

There was so much I wanted to say and I could tell she wanted to say more as well but it didn't seem like the right place or the right time. And then one of the nurses came in and said I should probably go because Mum needed to rest.

Devlin and his mum were waiting for me outside the door. I realised they were practically strangers and yet they'd come with me to the hospital and were about to take me home. Not that Devlin looked like a stranger; he was beginning to look pretty familiar by now, which was something I wasn't sorry about, especially when he flashed that smile of his at me. It was a pity he wasn't interested in me, I thought as we drove back to King Street, then berated myself for thinking such things at a time like this. But then I had to smile because it just meant I was human and it felt good.

Chapter Nineteen

Devlin's mum put me straight to bed when we got back. First, she went downstairs and got my things for me, like she knew I didn't want to face the empty flat by myself. And despite everything that had happened to me in one day, I fell asleep immediately and didn't wake up until the morning, which was a first for me since The Incident.

Devlin and I spent the morning together. We looked at Google Earth and he showed me Los Angeles and the house where he lived and the stadium where he went to watch baseball. I couldn't believe how big everything was. I swear the stadium car park was about the same size as the whole of Bath. Well, maybe not quite but it seemed that way. Also, I couldn't believe how all the streets were so straight and set out like a grid. Then we looked at Bath on Google Earth. They couldn't have been more different and

I began to understand how weird it must be for Devlin to leave that and come here.

Mum arrived home in the afternoon. She told me how she'd had her stomach pumped out but they hadn't been too hard on her because of the mitigating circumstances, even though she'd been admitted for alcohol poisoning and they usually took a pretty dim view of that. I wondered how Lily would have felt about being described as 'mitigating circumstances', but I didn't say anything.

I didn't go to the cinema today with Devlin, like we'd planned. I told him we'd have to do it another time because I needed to be with Mum. He told me to let him know when I was ready. Neither of us said anything but I knew that he knew about Lily and what had happened. I suppose his mum told him yesterday when we were at the hospital. I remembered how she'd asked me not to tell Devlin about it and realised that it must have been because of his aquaphobia. Life would be less complicated, I thought, if people were just up front about things, then you wouldn't get all these misunderstandings.

I thought it might be awkward when Mum got home and that we'd find it difficult to talk to each other but it wasn't like that. Mum looked a lot better and said she just felt like she had a bit of a hangover and if it wasn't for the drip they'd put her on last night she'd be a lot more hung over.

I knew she was trying to make light of a serious situation but I didn't mind. I'd just about forgiven her for scaring me so badly. She said she had to go to the supermarket so I went with her. It was a huge relief to be doing something so ordinary.

I kept thinking about Effy and how kind she'd been to me. I couldn't believe it was only yesterday. Anyhow, I thought I should text her to let her know I was okay and Mum said I should invite her round for the evening. Mum and I bought loads of silly things in the supermarket like popcorn and pizzas and she even let me get some Coke. I teased her when we got to the checkout about the fact that there wasn't a lentil or bean in sight.

When Effy had gone home, Mum went straight to bed and I went into my room. Suddenly the fun evening we'd just had dissolved away and I was overwhelmed by the heavy feeling of loss again. I looked at Lily's bed and all Lily's things and I didn't want to be in there. I got undressed and sat on the edge of my bed. I tried to picture Lily sitting in hers. I tried to have a conversation with her about everything that had happened today. But the spell had been broken; I couldn't pretend any more. I opened the front of the doll's house and picked up the Lily doll. I stroked the hair for little while and then I took the shoebox from under the bed and gently laid the doll in the box.

I went and climbed into Mum's bed, praying that she wouldn't tell me she was too tired to talk. Mum kissed me and we lay in silence for a long time listening to the ticking of her alarm clock. Mum's breathing was even and I thought she'd gone to sleep but when I looked I found her looking right back. Then, before that guilty feeling overwhelmed me, the one I get when I think Mum is wishing she was looking at Lily instead of me, Mum said, 'I'm so lucky to have you.'

She took my hand beneath the covers and squeezed it. 'I'm so proud of you, Milly, you've been so strong. And I'm sorry and ashamed that I haven't been there for you or been as strong as you.'

A tear rolled out of my eye and soaked into the pillow. I didn't feel very strong.

'You and Lily were always so different,' said Mum, 'even though you looked the same. I know Lily always seemed like the stronger one because she was so outgoing and she knew how to charm people, but she wasn't strong underneath, Milly. I sometimes wonder what would have happened if it had been the other way round . . . if it had been you who . . .' Mum's voice faltered. She couldn't bring herself to say the word so I squeezed her hand to let her know that I understood. She carried on, 'And I don't think we would have coped at all . . . I don't know what would have happened. I think I would have lost Lily as well.'

Mum stopped because she was crying. I think I understood what she meant. I think she was trying to say that, if it had been me who had drowned that day, Lily would have gone right off the rails. I think Mum was thinking that Lily would have found a different way to cope; maybe drinking or even drugs and that's how she'd have ended up losing both of us. I know neither of us wanted to believe that and it must have been hard for Mum to even nearly say it, but I think she was probably right.

'I know,' said Mum, 'because Lily was very like me and that's nearly the path I chose. But you're like the other part of me, the part that can be strong, and you've made me realise how foolish I've been.'

But I still didn't think I was strong and I thought Mum should know. I told her how I'd kept imagining Lily was still here; how I'd kept her alive in my head but I wasn't strong enough to keep it up and I didn't know what to do without her. I told her how I couldn't look in the mirror because I saw Lily and it hurt too much and I told her how I needed to do something about our bedroom so it didn't look as if Lily had just left it and might walk back in at any moment.

Of course there were things that I couldn't tell Mum, things that I couldn't put into words even to myself. Like that time on the beach in Wales, when I stopped Lily from doing stuff with that boy because I thought she was too young and should wait until she was older. Now I really wished I hadn't. Or about what had actually happened that day in April and how it was all my fault.

But it was as if Mum could read my mind.

'Promise me you'll never blame yourself for what happened that day,' said Mum. 'I couldn't bear it if your life was ruined by guilt. It's going to be hard enough living with the loss of your twin without the added burden of thinking it was anything but a tragic accident.'

We stopped talking for a time while we both thought about Lily. Then Mum said it wasn't going to get any easier; in fact it would probably get harder when the shock wore off, and she'd decided that it was time we both had some bereavement counselling. She said we could go together if I wanted and we mustn't hide any feelings we were having from each other. She said she'd help me with my room but she had to sort out some things first with her work. She was going to try and finish the book she was working on but she didn't think she could write any more Twin books after that. She'd been thinking about writing something else anyway but the publishers had wanted to stick with the Twins because they were still selling well. I fell asleep at that point.

Chapter Twenty

Of course I had to go back to school on the Monday after Mum's 'accident'. I felt sick with nerves all the way there. I felt sure that everyone would point at me and be whispering about what had happened, which was why I'd changed schools in the first place!

Effy met me at the gate and acted as if nothing had happened, which made me feel a whole lot better. And then I wondered what I'd been worrying about. Nobody was looking at me or whispering behind their hands. When we met up with Molly, Harriet and Katy at lunchtime, nobody brought up what had happened in the religious studies lesson. Everything would have been fine if it wasn't for the fact that I still had to face everyone in the next class on Friday. I tried not to think about it too much. I just wanted to get it over with but the week seemed to drag on and on like it was drawing out my agony on purpose.

In the end, I got through it without dying of embarrassment thanks to my friends. They sort of surrounded me as we went into the classroom. At first there was a slight lull in the conversation and people did look up, but Effy kept talking about what she was going to do at the weekend in that slightly loud voice of hers which, for once, I was grateful for.

There was a slightly awkward moment when Amy came in, but she avoided eye contact with me and the moment passed. But the best thing was that Mrs Clark didn't take the lesson. Instead, the other teacher, Mrs Granger, came back from maternity leave.

Although things were good at school, it wasn't so easy at home. The first big thing Mum and I had to face after our heart-to-heart was Christmas. Neither of us felt like celebrating but it's hard to ignore Christmas entirely. We talked about it because that's what we'd agreed: that we wouldn't hide what we were feeling. We decided that having Christmas alone in the flat would be too difficult so in the end we spent it on the farm in Cornwall.

It wasn't ideal, because the last time we were there Lily had been with us. But Mum said it was important to be among friends. I didn't tell her about the trick Lily had played on me and Mark that time because I didn't want her to think badly of Lily. But I was thinking about it all the way down there in the car, and I couldn't help smiling when I thought about how Lily had cut off her braids so she could pretend to be me and how she'd looked so funny when the hair had started to grow back in and she'd had two little tufts either side of her head for ages and ages.

I was nervous about seeing Mark again and I knew that I'd have to explain about what had happened, because I wanted him to know it hadn't been me who'd jumped on him and started kissing him.

He avoided me at first, but on the second day I tracked him down in the barn and just came straight out with it. He looked dead embarrassed, but I wasn't sure if it was because of what had happened or because I was talking about my dead sister. Some people get uncomfortable about that. But it sort of broke the ice between us and we got on okay after that, although we weren't as friendly as we had been two years ago.

Mum's friends weren't exactly celebrating Christmas, they were having a Yuletide celebration, but there were still presents and lots of nice food and Mum and I managed.

The other big thing we dealt with was my bedroom.

When I got home from school one day Mum said she had something for me. She took me into my bedroom and there, in the middle of the floor, was a big wooden box.

'It's a blanket box,' said Mum. 'I thought we could paint it and then you can choose some of Lily's special things and keep them in there. I've been in touch with Jeanie and she says we can put the rest in the attic.' Mum sounded nervous, like she wasn't sure how I was going to react or if it was the right thing to do.

'I think it's a great idea,' I told her, giving her a hug.

'Do you want me to help you?' said Mum.

'Okay,' I said.

I sort of wanted to do it on my own, but I thought it was important that Mum was there as well because it would be like saying goodbye to Lily again.

At first I wanted to put everything in the blanket box but it was impossible because it wasn't big enough. Mum had got some cardboard boxes for the attic and we started to put Lily's things into them. Every time I came across something I couldn't part with I put it in the wooden chest instead.

I won't pretend it was easy. It felt like I was packing Lily away, out of sight. I kept telling myself that it wasn't like that, because Lily would always be there but she'd be in me, in my heart and my memories, and that's what was important.

I know Mum was feeling the same way but we carried on until it was done.

I was clearing out under Lily's bed and I found a half-eaten bar of chocolate. I put it in one of the attic boxes along with Lily's clothes and toiletries and school books. One day Mum and I would have to deal with the contents of these boxes but it wouldn't be for a long time.

Meanwhile I chose the essence of Lily's life to keep in the special box. I put the scrapbook we'd made about our father at the bottom. I kept her knitted monkey, Bubbles, and her art book. Lily had been really good at art whereas I was better at maths and science.

There was an awful moment when I came across the blue hoodie in the back of the wardrobe. The one that the boy called Josh had put round my shoulders after the accident. I didn't want to have to explain to Mum where it had come from, so I folded it and placed it in one of the attic boxes.

I asked Mum if she minded the doll's house going up in the attic. I thought it was about time I got rid of it. Mum said that would be fine, so I got the box of dolls and took out the one that was Lily. I opened the front of the doll's house and took out the doll that was me and I placed them side by side in the blanket box. I took the journal that Ted had given to me, the one with Lily's and my life in it, and added it to the pile and then I shut the lid.

We got Devlin to help us carry everything else up to the top of the house. When I got back to my bedroom it looked so empty and sad that I thought I'd made the wrong decision. I suddenly wanted everything back, just as it had been, but there was no way I could do that after all the effort we'd gone to.

After that I spent most of my time in the sitting room and the kitchen and only went into my bedroom when it was time for bed. Mum must have noticed, because one weekend I went to stay with Effy and when I got home on the Sunday evening Mum was looking sheepish.

'I've done a couple of things to your room,' she said. 'I

hope you don't mind.'

The first thing I noticed was a sign stuck on the door. It said *Emily's Room*. I smiled at Mum who was hovering behind me. I couldn't believe it when I opened the door. Mum must have had some serious help to have got all this done in a couple of days. She'd painted the walls and everything!

I looked around. Mum had rearranged the furniture and there was even a new desk. She'd moved my bed and then she'd turned Lily's bed into a kind of sofa. It didn't have any bedding on it any more. Instead it was covered in a beautiful patchwork quilt, the sort of thing Lily would have loved, and there were plenty of cushions arranged along the back, against the wall. I noticed that one of the cushion covers was made from some of Lily's old clothes.

The whole thing was perfect. Everything about it said *Lily* in the best possible way. I knew I'd be able to use it to sit and relax or read a book and not feel sad any more when I looked at her empty bed.

'Do you like it?' said Mum. She was still looking worried.

'I love it,' I said, giving her a hug.

Devlin and I meet up with the others most Saturdays at the café. I always feel really relaxed with my new friends, because although they know about Lily and what happened, they never knew her so we don't talk about her. I don't mean that I don't want to talk about Lily, I just mean I can be myself when I'm with them and it's not all mixed up with who I used to be.

I've stopped going to Ted's and instead Mum and I see a grief counsellor twice a month, which really helps. There are a couple of things coming up which aren't going to be easy. First, it will be our birthday when I'll be turning fifteen. Mum and I are trying to decide what to do. There's a plaque at the crematorium with Lily's name on it and I expect we'll take her some flowers. Then a week later will be the anniversary of the accident. The counsellor asked us if we would be visiting the site where the accident happened and we said we wouldn't be going there. I think the pond was drained and it's on private land. I don't think going back there would help.

Mum said the best way for me to honour Lily was to make sure that I live a full and happy life. I know it won't be easy because Lily will always be with me and the older I get the further away she'll become, because she'll always be fourteen.

Chapter Twenty-one

Devlin came downstairs this afternoon to ask me if I wanted to go for a walk. The door between our flat and the rest of the house never got locked again after the thing with Mum, and I often go up there and play computer games with Devlin.

I was revising for a test at the time so I was glad of an excuse to stop. I poked my head round the door of Mum's workroom to tell her I was going out but I didn't elaborate because she was busy. She looked up from her work for a nanosecond, said, 'Fine, take care,' and carried on. She's not writing about twins any more, she's started a new book about a girl and her imaginary friend.

'Where are we going?' I asked Devlin when we got outside.

'I don't know,' he said.

'So we're just going to wander the streets, are we?'

'Yes, do you have a problem with that?'

'Why yes, I do,' I told him.

'So what would you like do?'

'Well,' I said, pretending to think for a second, 'I thought we might walk by the canal, or we could go on a river cruise, or to the Baths . . .' He was giving me a dangerous look. 'You really can't visit Bath without going to the Baths, you know. Or perhaps you'd like to go swimming?'

I easily avoided Devlin's hand when he tried to hit me because I was expecting it. I ran off down the street with Devlin in hot pursuit. There was a park up ahead and I dodged in there but he caught up with me easily and tackled me to the ground. We fell onto the grass laughing, and I was suddenly aware of how close Devlin was. His hand brushed mine as we lay side by side and my heart skipped a beat.

'Didn't your mother teach you not to mock the afflicted?' he said, bringing me back down to earth.

'Sorry, I couldn't resist it.'

He raised himself up on one arm and leaned over me. 'There's something I'm having trouble resisting,' he said and kissed me.

I screamed – and screaming is not good. Especially for the person who's got their lips pressed to yours. It was actually more of a squeak, but it was enough to make Devlin pull back sharply.

'Sorry . . .' he said, looking miserable and embarrassed.

'No . . .' I didn't know what to say or what was going on.

'I thought . . .' we both said at the same time.

Then he shut up and I blurted out, ' . . . you had a girlfriend back home.'

Now it was my turn to look embarrassed.

Devlin sat up. 'Why did you think that?'

'Because I'm stupid,' I said. I couldn't even remember why I'd thought it in the first place. I think I'd invented her because I thought Devlin didn't like me when in fact it was just the aquaphobia making him nervous. And then I'd held on to the idea because I was scared about how much I liked him and a mythical girlfriend seemed like a good excuse for the fact that nothing was going to happen between us. It all sounded completely crazy to me now and I laughed.

'It doesn't matter – obviously I was wrong,' I said, hoping he'd kiss me again.

'You were . . .' he said, moving in, his lovely blue eyes getting closer. I held my breath . . . and that's when it started to rain. And I mean rain. Without any warning, apart from the huge black cloud overhead which we'd failed to spot, despite the fact I was lying on my back staring up at it. Huge raindrops came pelting down. One hit me right in the eye. I squealed again. Devlin was on his feet. He grabbed my hand and pulled me up. Then we ran. Neither of us knew where we were running to. Devlin still had hold of my hand as we splashed through puddles that had instantly appeared.

There was a small building up ahead with an even

smaller porch – more of a recess really. We ran for it. There wasn't a lot of room, but by standing very close together we managed to get out of the rain.

Devlin's shirt was so wet it was sticking to his chest. The rain was running off my hair and collecting at the end of my nose. Devlin cupped my face in his hands and wiped the drop off with his thumb then pulled me towards him and he kissed me again, properly this time because I didn't scream.

It felt so good to have his fingers tangled in my hair and to feel the muscles on his back where my hands were wrapped round him. I tried to concentrate on the kiss and forget everything else, but my mind was racing and I couldn't stop it. Apart from the shock that Devlin was kissing me and that we'd just moved from being friends to something more, there was the old, familiar sense of guilt that I could be happy. This time I really didn't want to quash it. The thought of Lily was hovering at the back of my mind and I really didn't want to be thinking about Lily at a time like this.

Devlin pulled away. 'Are you okay?'

'I'm fine. More than fine . . . really.'

'Are you sure? I mean . . . if you'd rather we were just friends . . . I didn't mean to . . .'

'No.'

'I've wanted to do that since the first time I saw you,' he said.

'Really? But you never even spoke to me. I thought you hated me because your mum had made you talk to me . . .'

I was prattling again. It must have been nerves.

'I was just intimidated by how beautiful you looked,' he said.

I laughed. 'Don't be funny. I'm not beautiful.'

'Do all English girls have a problem with accepting compliments?' he said, putting his hands on my shoulders and giving me a fake stern look.

'No,' I told him. 'Only the stupid ones.'

'You're doing it again. Stop it. You're not stupid, you're beautiful.'

I laughed again. Who was I to argue?

'Do you ever stop laughing?' he asked.

'Not if I can help it,' I said, laughing.

'Well, let me help you,' said Devlin, covering my mouth with another kiss.

The rain had stopped, leaving a fresh, clean smell in the air.

'So what took you so long?' I asked Devlin as we walked hand in hand through the park.

'You mean before I made my move? Well . . .' Devlin paused, 'you were so sad and I didn't want to take advantage. That time when your mum was in the hospital and we came to get you . . .'

'I must have looked a right mess,' I interrupted, remembering how I'd cried on his shoulder.

'I really wanted to kiss you then but obviously I couldn't. I'd only just found out about your sister and I thought the last thing you needed was me making a move on you.'

I squeezed his hand. 'That was before Christmas.'

'I know, and you seem a lot better – no, happier now, so I thought it would be okay.' He stopped and turned me towards him, taking my other hand in his.

'You're sure it's okay?' he said, looking into my eyes.

I thought about answering that it was the best thing that had ever happened to me and that I was fine because I know that Lily would have told me to go for it. Instead, I took a step forward and gently pressed my lips to his. It was all the proof he needed and, as he kissed me back, I forgot about everything else except for the moment and Devlin's arms around me and his lips on mine. It was definitely the best kiss so far.

More books you'll love by Penelope Bush

Alice in time

If you could revisit your past, what would you see?

Things are at crisis point for fourteen-year-old Alice. Her mum is ruining her life, her dad's getting remarried, and Sasha, the most popular girl in school, hates her guts . . .

Then a bizarre accident happens, and Alice finds herself re-living her life as a seven-year-old through teenage eyes – and discovering some awkward truths. But can she use her new knowledge to change her own future?

'An amazing book.
Cleverly written, exciting and fast-paced.'
Chicklish

'An ambitious and successful novel.'
Books for Keeps

Diary of a Lottery Winner's Daughter

*'You've changed, Charlotte Johnson,
and if that's what having money does to people,
then I'm glad we haven't got any!'*
*I can't believe my best friend just said that.
It's so unfair. She thinks I've changed because of the money, but
I know I haven't. She's changed towards me.*

Charlotte hopes all her dreams can come true
when her mum wins £3.7 million on the lottery.
But being super-rich turns out to be a lot more
complicated than she'd expected . . .

'Funny, warm-hearted and sometimes frighteningly
honest, Penelope Bush goes beyond clichés and creates
quirky, truly believable characters with complicated lives.'
Julia Eccleshare, *Lovereading4kids*

piccadillypress.co.uk/teen

Go online to discover:

☆ more books you'll love

☆ competitions

☆ sneak peeks inside books

☆ fun activities and downloads

☆ Find us on Facebook for exclusive
competitions, giveaways and more!
www.facebook.com/piccadillypressbooks

☆ Follow us on Twitter
www.twitter.com/PiccadillyPress